EXIT WOUNDS

Exit Wounds

By Taylor Michaels

Copyright 2017 by Taylor Michaels

First Edition

ISBN-13: 978-1542660990

EXIT WOUNDS

TAYLOR MICHAELS

About the Author

Taylor Michaels writes romantic suspense and blames it entirely on all the Nancy Drew mysteries she read as a child. A technical support professional by day, she spends many nights writing stores where love blooms amidst danger and uncertainty. A long-time reader of romance books and thrillers, she loves the "oh my gosh, I didn't see that coming" plot twist almost as much as the happily-ever-after ending.

For more information please go to www.taylormichaels.com.

To learn more about upcoming books, get to participate in exclusive subscriber contests, and free content subscribe to Taylor's Newsletter today. Sign up forms are available on her website.

CHAPTER ONE

"Morning, Laura."

The brunette receptionist for Sonoran Security Agency glanced up from her computer screen and gave Ian Randall the once over. His stomach knotted, just the way it always had when inspections had been made in the Army. Had the shower, coffee and aspirin succeeded in giving the illusion to the outside world of normal? He detected a trace of approval in her eyes before she smiled. "Good morning, Ian."

He forced a smile in return and uttered a silent prayer of thanks that he had managed to appear calm. The knots twisting his stomach all morning eased.

"Shawn asked to see you when you got in," Laura said.

His stomach twisted again with a vengeance.

"Okay," Ian replied as he opened the door to the back offices and strode down the hallway.

What had I been thinking? He'd almost finished off the bottle of whiskey before falling into his bed. Ian knew he should've stopped last night, but the numbness felt too good. Nope, getting drunk wasn't about feeling good. It was about not feeling at all, and last night Jack Daniels delivered.

A faint essence of déjà vu hit him as he traveled the hallway of never-ending paint on drywall. He thought of the buildings he been in in Iraq. Almost the same. No pictures, billboards, or art, just stark naked walls.

Morgan, Shawn's girlfriend, had been lobbying for putting up some artwork, but so far, hadn't made any inroads on that front. *Geez, Shawn. Maybe Morgan has a point on this one.*

He arrived at his brother's office. He took a short breath and then knocked on the closed door.

"Come in," Shawn replied.

Ian opened the door and found his brother behind his desk studying papers. Shawn looked up, then gestured at the chair across from his desk. "Close the door and have a seat."

Ian sank into the chair slowly.

Shawn studied him in silence. "How's it going?"

Oh great, here we go again. Ian forced another smile while silently cursing his brother's all-too-keen observation skills. "Fine. It's going fine."

Shawn leaned back in his chair, and trained his gaze back to Ian, staring directly eye-to-eye. "Are you sure?"

Ian took a deep breath. "Well, it's been a bit of an adjustment. I did two tours in Iraq before I started here three months ago. It's a big change from the army, but it's coming along."

Shawn nodded. "New apartment okay?"

"Yeah." Ian nervously straightened his jacket. "Why all the questions?"

Shawn's smile faded. "When you first came home, you stayed with mom and dad, and then came out to Phoenix and stayed with me. The man who bunked at my place was different from the man who enlisted eight years ago."

Irritation crackled through Ian. "Really? War will do that for you, bro."

Shawn fingered his pen as his brow dipped into a frown. "Yeah. No question about that. Any more nightmares?"

Ian took a deep breath. "Not any of your business."

"Actually, it is," Shawn replied quietly. "We've got a new client and I want to put you on this case. You are perfect for this. Provided you have your head on straight."

Ian raised his chin. "I can handle it."

His brother studied him. Then he crooked a grin, and if Ian didn't know any better, he swore he'd caught a mischievous gleam in his eye. "Glad to hear that. Come with me."

Shawn stood up and walked around the desk. "Our client has hired us to find her brother. He appears to have gone AWOL."

Ian did his best not roll his eyes at his brother's attempt to insert a little military jargon in the conversation. Shawn was a great guy. Hard-working, a shrewd judge of character, but he'd never served in the military, and from time to time, he'd try out terminology or attempt to make Ian believe he knew what it was like in the Middle East. Most attempts were an epic fail in Ian's eyes.

He rose from his seat and followed Shawn to the door. "She's with Matt right now."

Ian walked at his brother's side down the hallway and almost unconsciously matched Shawn's stride to Matt Anderson's office. A sense of familiarity settled over Ian. *Relax. It's muscle memory. Nothing more.*

Just before they reached the door, Shawn stopped and touched Ian on the arm. "She's upset, and, I suspect, in denial. She's going to need someone who is patient, focused, and a bit of a diplomat. I have complete confidence that you will be able to get along with her."

Ian nodded. "Got it." Shawn opened the door and entered the room, took a couple steps, and moved aside to usher Ian in.

Her back was to him and what registered to Ian first was her long, brown hair styled into a conservative ponytail. She hadn't turned to look at them, yet something about her seemed familiar.

Matt stood up from behind his desk and prepared to make introductions. She turned and smiled at Shawn before training her gaze on him. Her eyes widened in surprise.

Ian froze and his jaw tightened. It was all that he could do to not throttle Shawn for not warning him as to what he was walking into. Ian swallowed. "Hello, Jillian. Long time no see."

The surprise in her golden-brown eyes quickly banked, to be replaced with a calm, reserved expression. But there was something else, another emotion, he couldn't quite get a fix on. *Caution?*

Whatever it was, the fun, easy-going girl he'd taken to prom and homecoming in high school was long gone. Before him stood a woman who looked stressed. From the faded lipstick to the tight grip she had on her handbag that rested in her lap, Jillian appeared years older than her actual age of twenty-nine years.

Her demure hair style complimented a tasteful, yet expensive business suit. The skirt was a modest length, followed by sensible, low-heeled dress shoes, and a spectacular set of legs. *Well, at least that hadn't changed.* He swallowed and his thoughts lingered of times long ago and of places his eyes couldn't--scratch that--shouldn't check out. As he looked back at her face, a soft blush bloomed on her cheeks, almost as if she'd read his thoughts. Jillian glanced back at Matt, put her hand up to her face, and wiped her nose with a tissue.

Great, she's been crying. Shawn should have warned me she was an emotional basket case.

"Jillian, I believe you know Shawn and Ian Randall," Matt then added.

"Yes." She extended her free hand and shook Shawn's first without comment, and then Ian's. Jillian said softly, "Hi, Ian."

As their fingers touched, Ian could swear that electricity literally crackled up his arm. Ian swallowed and shook her hand, squeezing it gently before releasing it. Avoiding his gaze, she yanked her hand back as if he'd pinched her fingers.

Matt cleared his throat. "Ms. Connors came home two nights ago and found her condo robbed and her brother missing. She filed a burglary and missing person's report with the authorities, but feels that a greater effort needs to be made to find her brother."

"Wesley is missing?" Ian asked.

Jillian bit her lower lip and nodded.

"Why don't you give us the details of what's happened," Shawn said as he and Ian sat down in nearby chairs.

"Where should I start?"

"Start with when you came home and found your place robbed," Matt replied.

Ian couldn't quite be sure, but it appeared to him that Matt's southern drawl was just a tad more noticeable than it had been a few moments before. He cast a quick glance over at Matt and saw a polite, professional expression on his face.

Jillian took a deep breath. "You'll have to forgive me, but I've never done this before." She paused before adding, "I mean, hiring a detective firm."

Ian wanted to correct her, but said nothing. Sonoran Security was more in the asset protection business, like security guards and electronic surveillance. Private investigation wasn't actually the type of business they took on...until now, it seemed. But since Jillian had known both Ian and Shawn from years ago, he chalked up the acceptance of this case as more of a personal favor for an old acquaintance.

"I own and operate a venue-for-hire facility called La Villa de Gardena. Most of our business comes from wedding receptions and company parties. Two nights ago, I came home late and my condo had been robbed. The thieves took my TV, stereo, jewelry, you know, stuff like that. I had thought that when I got home my brother, Wesley, would have already been there. But he wasn't. After I called the police, I called and texted him several times. But he never called back or responded. And no one has seen him since that day."

"So I take it that your brother resides with you. What does he do for a living?" Shawn asked.

"He's a sales representative for a liquor distributor. They sell to restaurants, some wine shops, bars, even casinos."

"How long has he worked for them?" Ian asked.

"About five months." Jillian locked eyes with Ian for a few seconds and looked away.

Ian leaned back in his seat and studied her. The Jillian he knew never had a good poker face and apparently that part of her personality hadn't changed. She was hiding something. Part of him wanted to dig deeper and ask more questions. But he could tell from Shawn and Matt's silence they wanted her to continue to talk, so he'd wait.

"The police pointed out that the house wasn't broken into. The doors were locked and the windows intact. They believe that he…." Jillian paused and even from a few yards away, Ian could see the shudder roll through her as she struggled to finish the sentence.

She swallowed, and began to play with the tissue in her hand. After a moment, she quietly said, "They think that he took the stuff and moved out."

Jillian glanced up and gave each man a concerned look. "But he didn't. Then yesterday, I got a phone call from a man who was looking for Wesley. He didn't say exactly why when I pressed for more details, but my brother is in trouble. I--I can sense it." Her voice cracked with desperation. "You have to find him."

"Have you reached out to his employer to see if Wesley's shown up for work?" Shawn asked her.

She nodded. "His employer said Wesley asked to take off a couple of personal days. That's weird. Wesley never mentioned it to me."

Ian cleared his throat, and she looked at him. "I'm going to apologize for asking this question, but I believe it needs to be asked. Why is Wes living with you? He's got to be what, twenty-seven, twenty-eight? Right?"

Her eyes took on a definite deer-in-the-headlights aspect as if his question had caught her off guard. Then Jillian nodded.

"He's twenty-six." She looked down at the crumpled tissue in her hands. "Wes got into problems in college. He joined a fraternity and it was a hard-partying group. I'm afraid that he started using drugs and became addicted. He left college and with the family's support, he went into rehab. He completed the program and has been sober since. He didn't want to go back to college so he started a career. He was just getting his feet under him, and I expected that he'd be moving out in the next few months." Jillian locked eyes with him after she finished as if, despite the casual delivery of her explanation, she looked like she was prepared for some comment from him about Wesley's fall from sobriety.

"Are you sure that your brother hasn't had a relapse?" Matt asked.

"I can't be one hundred percent certain, but I would think that if something like 'that' was going on, I'd sense it."

"Okay." The tall Texan shot a skeptical glance at Shawn and then at him.

Ian doubted that she'd be able to sense it. He'd seen his fair share of people with drug issues, and it was amazing how long people could hide stuff like that until things completely fell apart.

Shawn shifted in his chair and leaned forward. "Have you checked in with some of his friends? Do you know where he likes to hang out, when he's not working or with you?"

"No, I haven't. I'd hoped that this would all be a big mistake, that he'd walk in and talk about how the car broke down, wasn't able to get a cell phone connection, or something like that."

Her voice trailed off and she pulled out another tissue from her handbag.

Matt softly cleared his throat. "Jillian, you mentioned that yesterday you got a phone call and that someone is searching for your brother. Do you have any idea why?"

"No. I asked who he was and why, and the man wouldn't answer."

"Okay," Shawn replied. "I want to put Ian with you for the next couple days. He'll be there to look for clues as to what's been going on. We'll follow those leads down and work to find your brother."

For the first time since Ian had met her, Jillian flashed a smile. "Thanks. What now?"

"Are you planning to return to work after this?" Ian asked.

"Yes, I have a wedding and reception the day after tomorrow. There's quite a bit of last minute preparation that needs to be done."

"Good, it's time you go back to work. We'll pull the team together and begin to search for Wesley."

***

Jillian forced herself to walk with slow deliberate steps to her car. *Breathe. It will be fine. Just breathe.* The mental pep talk did little to tamp down the urge to make a full-on sprint to her car.

What had she'd been thinking? Hiring Sonoran Security to find her missing brother had seemed like a prudent idea at the time. She'd assumed that by knowing Shawn and Ian from high school, she'd ensure some discretion by using their agency. Last time she heard, Ian was still in the military. When had he returned home and went to work in his brother's business?

High school sweethearts. The term sounded so quaint, even

a bit old-fashioned. She opened the door and slid into the driver's seat, tossing her handbag over on the passenger seat. Jillian sank back into the seat, looked up to the upholstered roof and closed her eyes.

Ian. He's back. She would have sworn that she'd never see him again. Today when he spoke, he was cool and analytical in his comments and tone. What a far cry from the anger and the hurt when they last spoke years ago. He'd accused her of seeing another men. It wasn't true, but no matter how much she denied it, he didn't believe her.

Jillian opened her eyes and took in a deep, slow breath. Now, after all these years, he was back and trying to find Wesley. She leaned forward and inserted the key into the ignition and turned on the engine. The soft hum of the engine mirrored the nervous buzz coursing through her. As she slowly backed out of the parking space she wondered how working with Ian while they searched for her brother would work out.

For what it was worth, Ian appeared as surprised to see her as she'd been to see him. Of course, that hadn't stopped him from checking her out, and Jillian had picked up a fleeting expression of appreciation.

She pressed her lips together and inhaled before opening her lips and slowly pushing out her breath. Ian had matured over the years. The tall, lanky young man she had dated in school had filled out. Even under the well-tailored suit it wasn't hard to miss that he'd added some muscle. She'd heard he'd joined the military and served in the Middle East. Jillian recalled the old phrase, "War is hell." Given the stories reported on the evening news, she had no doubt he'd seen a fair amount of destruction and conflict. But something was different about him. A subtle aura of weariness clung to him.

Of course, the distrust in his eyes was still there. She'd have to be blind to have missed that.

Chapter Two

Ian pulled into the parking space at La Villa de Gardena later that afternoon and turned off the ignition. *Wow!* The word didn't even begin to cover the shock that hit him as he surveyed the facility that sat outside his car's front window. How did Jillian Connors get the money to own this?

Jillian has so matter-of-factly mentioned that she owned and ran a place to host events. He'd assumed it was a small hall. Some basic facility that hosted fraternal organizations during the week, and served up fish fry dinners on Friday nights followed by bingo. Thank goodness he had kept his thoughts to himself, because if La Villa de Gardenia was any indication of what to expect, Jillian had done well in business.

As he walked to the entrance, the sound of water broke the silence. Inside the front gate, a massive fountain sat in the middle of the courtyard. In the shadows beyond the yard he spied thick oak doors which led to what Ian supposed had to be meeting and banquet rooms.

A man stood on a ladder across the courtyard, making adjustments to the lights, which hung from the trees.

"Excuse me. I'm here to meet with Jillian Connors. Do you know where I can find her?"

The man glanced down at him and smiled. "Yes, she is in the large reception room." The man pointed to the covered walkway to Ian's right. "There's a carved wooden door you'll enter. Once inside, turn left and go down the hallway. You can't miss the room."

"Thank you."

Ian walked across the courtyard and entered the building. He didn't need to do much more than follow the workmen bringing in rolling carts with chairs and tables. He stopped at the entrance of the ballroom. Jillian stood over to the left talking with another woman as they hovered over a large clipboard. She then began to direct the placement of the furniture.

Ian rapidly amended his first impression of Jillian. He'd probably been a bit quick to judge. Having a missing brother, a robbery, and a cryptic phone call from a mysterious man would more than likely push anyone emotionally to the edge. But watching her direct the team of workers on where to set up the furniture, her organization and focus were admirable. The sun streamed through the bank of windows, causing her hair to glow to a golden brown. Still bound in a demure pony tail, he wondered if she ever wore it loose like when she was in high school with him years ago. He took a slow, deep breath and held it before exhaling. *Hands off. She's a client and after all these years she's probably moved on.*

Jillian looked over at him, touched the lady on the arm and

said something to her before she handed over the clipboard and walked over to him.

"Hi. You're finally here," Jillian said.

Ian frowned as he picked up a slight rebuke in her greeting. Exactly when was she expecting him to arrive? After she'd left the office, the staff met for more than an hour mapping out the next steps that needed to be taken to find her brother.

"Sorry. It took a little longer than we planned to get the assignments to the team."

"Oh," Jillian replied.

Her one word response had a subtle skeptical tone to it and for some reason, irritation started to bubble within him.

"It didn't sound as if you were in any physical danger," Ian added. "If that had been the case, we would have handled it differently. I would have followed you from the office."

With that comment, the small forced smile on her face evaporated like water on hot summer concrete.

Ian wished the moment the words left his lips that he could reel them back in. He sounded like a defensive jerk. What had his brother said earlier about diplomacy?

Jillian glanced at the woman holding the clipboard and watching the workers set up the tables and chairs.

"She's the wedding planner," Jillian said. "She's good. I'll be here at least another thirty minutes going over things before I can break off. Would you like to wait in my office?"

"If it's not a problem, I'd like to walk around and get a feel of the facility."

"Okay, if you get lost, or need to find my office, just ask any of the crew."

This time she smiled warmly at him. "Thirty minutes?"

"Got it," Ian replied.

She turned and walked back to the wedding planner who'd begun to direct the crew to move the tables around a bit.

Ian stepped into the interior hallway and glanced around. Which way now? Ian laughed softly. It didn't matter, just as long as he wasn't late arriving at Jillian Connor's office in thirty minutes.

By the time he had explored the property, Ian had concluded that running a facility of this size and scale was like running a military base. There were grounds, storage rooms, kitchens, ready rooms for guests, large ballrooms, small meeting rooms, and even a small chapel.

He figured Jillian's facility bought a lot of alcohol and that may have factored in her brother being hired by a liquor distributor. A place like this probably had an annual tab that easily could rival most neighborhood bars.

He stood at her open office door. Jillian was studying a computer screen.

"Are you ready to talk?"

She glanced up and nodded. "Sure. Have a seat."

Ian sank into the leather chair in front of her desk and waited as she logged off. He looked around the room. The office was tastefully decorated, but he'd expected to see some photos. A boyfriend, husband, maybe children, but there was nothing in view. *Was there anyone in her life right now?*

"What do you want to talk about?" Jillian asked.

Ian glanced back at her. She appeared calm and her question on the surface seemed innocuous enough; however, he picked up a trace of defensiveness in the tone of her voice. "Tread carefully," the voice in his head reminded.

"I want to get a handle on who Wesley is. That way we'll get a better idea of where to search for him. So tell me more about him."

"Okay, exactly what do you want to know?"

"Simple stuff. For example, what are his hobbies, what does he do in his downtime?"

She sat back in her seat and took a deep breath. "Well, Wes was a huge sports fan, and I mean huge. I would leave on Saturday or Sunday mornings and head to work, and when I came back at the end of the day, I'd find him still parked in front of the TV."

"Did he have favorite teams?"

"Probably. I'm not into sports, so I've never paid much attention. The Arizona Cardinals, I guess."

"What's his favorite sport? Football, baseball, or basketball?"

Jillian pressed her lips together and shook her head. "Honestly, he appeared to like them all. I know this sounds strange because everyone has a favorite team, right? But Wes didn't have any team jerseys or season tickets to any of the local teams. But he amazed me. He could rattle off the scores of the games played during the weekend like a machine." Her expression darkened. "Exactly, where is your line of questioning going, Ian?"

"Trying to get a sense of who he is."

Jillian reached over, took a sip from a diet soda and ran her finger up and down the side of the can as she pondered what to say next. She sighed softly.

"My brother is a good man, but he's not the best judge of character. In college, he hung out with people who partied hard, and he followed along and got into trouble. He cleaned up his act. He stayed with me while he got his career going."

"Okay."

She shifted in her chair and the leather softly creaked before she locked eyes with his. "I think you need to understand that most weekends I wasn't at home with him. In a business like this, many events take place on weekends."

Jillian gently rubbed her forehead. "I don't want you to think I didn't care about my brother, because I can't tell you who his favorite sports team was."

"Didn't care?"

Her head snapped up. "What?"

"You said, 'didn't care.'" Ian waited and let the silence hang in the air.

It didn't take long. Anger flashed in her eyes. "I love my brother and I believe he's in danger, and we need to find him. It's as simple as that. Clear?"

"Crystal clear." Ian sat back in the seat, and racked his brain, and searched for a neutral question to defuse the situation. What he really needed was more personal information, but to pursue this line of questioning would get him nowhere for the time being.

"Okay, tell me about you. This place is extraordinary. How long have owned it and how did you get into this line of business?"

Her frown melted. "I've owned it for four years. When I graduated from college, I started working at one of the major resorts, booking their events. I liked it and was good at it. But over time, I wanted to be at a venue which could provide a bit more romance and intimacy. Weddings are a once in a lifetime event. They should be special. The large hotels and resorts in town are nice, but there is a cookie-cutter element to having your reception there. La Villa de Gardenia does not provide a cookie-cutter experience."

Ian smiled. Jillian practically glowed as she talked about her facility. "It's large. With the parking space, it's four or five acres, right?"

"Ten."

"How did you find the funding for this?"

"My grandmother. When she died, I inherited some money. I purchased the land and built it from scratch."

"Must have been a large amount."

Jillian paused before answering, leaving Ian with the impression that she was uncomfortable with disclosing too much information on her finances. "It was substantial. But I do have a mortgage on this place, if that is what you're thinking. I hope to have it paid off in a few years."

"Is your family still here in Phoenix?"

"No. Mom and Dad moved back to the Bay Area."

Ian watched her as she spoke. She'd stopped stroking the diet soda can and leaned back in her chair. "How did they handle Wesley's addiction issue?"

"They were very upset and worried and wanted to blame the whole thing on his friends. But they've supported him going to rehab and are very proud of the progress that he's made."

"I walked around for a while, and even pulled one of the brochures off one of the tables in the hallway, but I didn't go into any places that didn't have an open door. Do you have time to give me a tour?"

Jillian grinned. "Sure." She rose from her chair and straightened her jacket before coming around the desk. He rose from the chair. As she got closer to him he noticed that she appeared to keep a small distance between them. As if she was deliberately staying out of reach. *Yep, she's not interested is anything more than finding her brother. When this is over, you'll probably never see her again.* Disappointment washed through him as he realized that at some level a part of him had hoped for something more.

Clearing her throat, she smiled. "Let's start with a quick tour of the reception rooms, and then go to the kitchen."

"Okay," Ian responded.

For the next twenty minutes, they traveled from room to room, with Jillian pointing out the ballrooms which ranged from small rooms suitable to dinner parties to one capable of hosting an event of several hundred. They had finished a quick tour of the kitchen facilities and were in the hallway back to her office, when Jillian's cell phone rang.

She looked at the cell phone and reached up and tugged at the end of her ponytail. "I don't recognize the number. Excuse me, this could be a customer." She picked up. "Good afternoon, La Villa de Gardena. How can I help you?" After a moment, her face paled and her gaze traveled over to Ian. "Who is this?"

CHAPTER THREE

Jillian gulped, and the fear sluiced through her veins like ice water. She glanced over at Ian. If she had meant to sound authoritative or strong, it fell short on all counts. The words creaked out of her, sounding more like a whisper.

"Ms. Connors, you can call me Joe. I'm looking for Wesley. Where is he?"

Joe. The name drew a blank. Wesley had never mentioned anyone by that name, so why was this man searching for her brother? She glanced over at Ian.

"Keep talking," he mouthed.

She nodded. "Joe."

"Speaker phone," Ian whispered. Jillian nodded, tried to punch the button to change to a broadcast mode, but stopped. How did she do that? If she bungled it up she might hang up on the caller and that could make things worse. She glanced back at Ian and whispered, "Don't know how."

Ian moved closer and Jillian moved the phone away from her face so he could hear. "You were the man who called me just recently looking for Wes, right?"

"Yes. Your brother and I were supposed to meet."

"About what?" Jillian asked.

"Oh come on, Ms. Connors, don't try to play innocent with me. You know what this is about."

Jillian shook her head. "I'm afraid I don't. My brother's disappeared. My house was ransacked, things taken, and you think that I know what's going on. You're misinformed."

"Wesley owes me money. Fifty thousand dollars to be precise. He was supposed to make the first payment two days ago and he never showed."

Fifty thousand dollars! Air whooshed from her lungs in a loud gasp. "You're lying."

"No. It's the truth, and I want my money." Joe's clipped, cold tone scared her more than if he'd shouted or screamed at her. She struggled with a reply. The seconds ticked.

"Ms. Connors, are you there?" Joe asked firmly

"Y—yes," Jillian stammered.

She had to think of something. "Um… you have me at a disadvantage. I… I don't know what you are talking about."

The man on the other end of the line whispered a curse. "Ask your brother."

"I would if I knew where he was."

"Jillian, I think you know where he is. I want my money and soon. Tell Wesley that if he doesn't make his payment soon, I will take action."

"Please, I really don't know what you're talking about, and

I can't find my brother. Unless you know where he is, and you're playing some sick game."

"Then you'd better find him." Joe replied. "Or make good for him. You aren't as clueless as you claim. I have your signature on the loan."

"Co-signed? I've never co-signed for a loan for Wesley."

The caller recited a list of facts about Jillian that left her standing there in slack-jawed silence. Name, home address, business address, annual revenue made from the business, tax return information, and her social security number. He finished the list by saying, "Wesley owes the money. If you insist on saying that he's disappeared, okay. But that doesn't change the fact that you co-signed for a loan." Joe exhaled, leaving her with the impression that he was weary of her denial. "I don't care who pays the loan, just as long as I get paid."

"It can't be mine." She glanced over at Ian who was staring at the phone. He looked up at her and she saw rage in his eyes. Fearing that he may explode, Jillian reached up and placed her hand on his chest.

"Take it up with your brother. I'll wait a bit longer, but not much."

The man disconnected the call and Jillian lowered the phone and looked at Ian before covering her mouth with her other hand.

"Jillian?" She dropped her hand from her mouth. The anger had faded and concern graced his face.

She didn't reply. What had Wesley gotten himself into? This had to be a huge mistake. Yet, Joe what-ever-his-name-is knew a lot about her finances. Far too much for this to be a bluff. Wesley must have provided this information, but why?

"Hey." Ian placed both of his hands on her shoulder. They were gentle and even with a jacket on heat slowly worked its way to her. "Look at me."

Her eyes misted over. "Give me a few minutes."

Ian stepped back. "I'll come back in a bit."

Jillian closed her eyes against the tears. She sensed him stepping back, then leaving. She swallowed, opened her eyes, scanned the empty hallway, and crossed her arms over her chest. *Wesley, where are you and what have you done?*

***

Ian stuck his head through Jillian's office door. "Ready to talk?"

"Yes. Come in," Jillian replied.

He entered quietly and sank down in the chair in front of her desk. Jillian took a few moments to truly study Ian. The lanky boy from high school had matured. His hair was cut short, and just a trace of a five o'clock shadow graced his jaw. Her gaze traveled to his hands and noted the absence of a wedding ring. But she wondered briefly if he was or had been.

Lord knows it had been a long time, over a decade, since they'd last seen each other. A lot could happen in that amount of time. Look at what she'd done, and she'd bet a steak dinner, he had a story to tell as well.

Jillian tamped down the urge to smile. When she'd caught him checking her out a few hours ago, she'd have to admit, it felt nice to be...noticed. It seemed like it has been an eternity since a man had done that.

Jillian chewed on her bottom lip, picked up a pen from her

desk, and rolled it between her fingers as she considered what to say.

She cleared her throat. "As you heard, this man believes I've taken out a loan for fifty thousand dollars."

When he arched an eyebrow, she added, "I never took out a loan. Maybe Wesley, unable to get a loan himself, decided use my identity."

"What makes you say that?"

Jillian didn't answer immediately. Ian's question was a reasonable one. His tone was calm, logical, yet why did she feel as if he suspected that she had some hand in this whole mess? She straightened in her chair and locked gazes with him. The voice in her head warned her to take a breath and reply in a cool, intellectual manner. "Because this man has information about me and my business he shouldn't have unless someone shared it, and I didn't provide it to him."

"Why would Wesley take out a loan for fifty thousand?"

She set the pen down on the desk, stared at it, and then sighed. "Great question." She grimaced. "Honestly, Ian, I have no idea why he would borrow such a sum."

"Okay. Let's pull the number off your cell. I'll give it to the team at the office and we'll see what we can find out about this guy."

"Fine." Jillian picked up her mobile phone, wrote the number down on a post-it note, and handed it over.

***

Ian looked at the post-it note, grabbed his cell phone, and started to stand up. "I'm going to step out for a minute and check in with the office and give them the phone number."

"No. Stay. Use my office. The crew should have completed setting up the banquet hall. I need to review things. I'll be back shortly."

Jillian stood up, straightened her jacket, and left the room. He sat still and deliberately didn't turn to watch her leave. Once he heard the door click, he dialed the main line. Laura, the receptionist picked up on the third ring. "Sonoran Security."

"Laura, it's Ian. I'm checking in and have some information I need the team to investigate."

"Hi, Ian. Matt and Shawn are out. Do you want either of their voice mails?"

"Yeah, patch me through to Shawn's."

"Hang on."

Within seconds his brother's voice mail box greeting began and after the beep, Ian left a brief recap of what had happened and also left the phone number. "Shawn, when you get this message, please give me a call back. Thanks."

Ian ended the call and briefly considered calling back to see if Laura could patch him into the tech team. They were the ones who did everything from background searches to wiring of security systems. If he was able to speak with someone there, maybe they could research the number and get back with a quicker answer.

His phone rang and he looked at the number. *Shawn.* Ian answered his phone. "That was quick."

"Yep, I'm going to forward the phone number to Sabrina and Paul, and they'll look into it. If we can get some information on who this man is, we may have a clue as to what is going on. How is our client coping?"

Client. The word jarred Ian. He'd spent the last few hours with his former high school sweetheart pretending that everything was just business. Trust his brother to put things in proper perspective.

"Fine. A little defensive about Wesley. When I inquired about hobbies and interests, she seemed a little clueless. She even realized it and got a bit irritated. The phone call rattled her, but she rallied."

"What is your take on this?" Shawn asked.

"Honestly, I'm not sure. Wesley Connors has definitely gotten into some trouble and I think he may be on the run or hiding out, but what caused this, is anyone's guess."

"Well, let's see what the tech team can turn up. How are you holding up?"

Ian sat back down in the seat and stared up at the ceiling. "Fine, Shawn. I'm fine. But, you should have warned me that our 'client' was Jillian before I walked into the room. You blindsided me."

His response was greeted with silence on the other line. "Point made. If you knew it had been Jillian, would you have taken the case?"

Ian paused. *Would he have taken it?* "Touché. To be sure, I don't know."

"Okay. If we get anything tonight, I'll have someone call. If not, stop by the office tomorrow morning for the staff meeting at eight-thirty."

"Got it."

Ian punched the disconnect button and stared at the ceiling. Shawn's decision to not warn him the client was his former girl-friend was a serious breach of the code of conduct. You didn't set up your buddies to be blindsided. When this case was over, he'd have to have a man-to-man talk with his brother.

A light knock on the door interrupted his thoughts. Ian straightened in his chair. "Come on in."

Jillian popped in. "All done?"

"Yeah, for the time being. They're going to check the number."

A small smile broke on Jillian's lips. "Great."

"We'll see. We may not find anything on this guy, and he could be using a burner phone."

Her smile faded. Ian's gut tightened. His direct answer let her down, and despite all the years which had transpired, hurting her still didn't settle well with him.

"I'm getting ready to go home. Is there anything else we need to talk about?" Jillian asked.

She turned off the desk lamp and gathered her purse. "No. Are you going to be okay?"

Jillian glanced up. "Sure."

Her answer was light, soft, forced and not the truth. Jillian was many things but a good liar was not one of them. Today's call had rattled her. Maybe that was a good thing. He sensed she knew more than she revealed. But why? Jillian desperately wanted to find her brother.

She appeared to ignore him as she pulled her keys from her purse and locked her desk. Once finished, she glanced at him and caught his stare.

"What?"

"Nothing."

Ian rose from his chair. "Let me walk you to your car. Go straight home and lock up once you're inside. If this guy calls again, don't answer. Let it go to voice mail. Maybe he'll leave a message with more information we can follow up on."

She walked around the desk and walked past him to the office door. Exhaustion dimmed her brown eyes. All the adrenaline fueling her for the past few days had finally washed out of her system.

"I'm parked out back."

He followed her, and she stopped and turned so quickly that he almost ran over her. Jillian took a step back, putting at least an arm's distance between them, and forced a small, weary smile.

"Thanks for your support. I've not been the easiest person to work with today. I'm sorry."

"No. You've been great," Ian said. Silence hung in the air. He was at a loss of what to say or do next. The thought pinged through his mind that maybe she needed a hug. Heck, right now he could use one, but he was certain given her disapproving looks when she caught him checking her out, if he hugged her, Jillian might scramble out of his arms like a scared rabbit.

"Let's get you in your car and on the way home," he said quietly.

Jillian nodded. They traveled in silence to her car, stopping only to lock doors and turn off lights. Once inside her BMW, she turned on the motor, and, as the soft click of the door lock registered, she glanced at him. Uncertainty graced her face, as if she was debating what to say. Seconds passed before she mouthed, "Good night" and then drove off.

Ian stood and watched as the car crossed the parking lot and pulled onto the street merging with eastbound traffic. The rear headlights dimmed as the car faded into the twilight.

A sense of emptiness settled on him and it felt like the cool of an evening chill. He shoved his hands into his pockets and rooted for his keys. He was an idiot. Jillian had clearly moved on with her life and once this case was over, he needed to do the same.

Chapter Four

Ian stepped through the apartment doorway as a large gust of wind whipped into the entryway and sent a couple of dried bougainvillea leaves in after him. Shrubbery along the walkway and the large eucalyptus tree near the front entrance shook against the coming storm. The keys clicked a protest when he tossed them and the mail against the kitchen counter. The low growl of thunder followed. Within seconds rain drops splattered lightly on the windows. He turned his attention to the mail in front of him, consciously trying to ignore the storm. For some reason, he couldn't quite explain, the wind and thunder made him edgy.

A loud crack of thunder broke, and he physically winced. His chest tightened, and he struggled for breath. Images and thoughts flooded his mind, and suddenly he was there. Smoke, screaming, men shouting commands, and a fuzzy sense of shock and confusion.

"Oh God, not again." He tossed the mail aside and clenched

the counter with both hands as he slowly drew in a calming breath and exhaled. All it took was something, a sound, smell, or thunder, and he was there.

While still taking in slow controlled breaths, he stared at the framed print which hung over the sofa in the living room. The image featured a small wooden cottage in the woods, pine trees, and a snow-capped mountain in the distance. *Focus on the image. Put yourself in the picture. Hear the water in the stream and the bird's song?*

Ian's chest loosened a notch, and he lurched over, grasping a dish towel, and wiped his brow. He laid the cloth down on the counter with trembling hands. Thunder growled in the distance. If this storm continued, this would be a long night. He stepped over to the cabinet and opened the door. Good, he had at least half a bottle. He set the whiskey on the counter, and then searched for a glass. *Ice would be nice.* He preferred his Jack on ice, but to heck with it. He didn't feeling taking the time to get it. Instead, he poured a few ounces into the glass, then downed it.

The taste, heat, and kick registered. He went to the refrigerator and hit the ice dispenser button with his glass. Ice rattled into the glass. Then he poured about two fingers worth. Lifting his drink, he watched the liquid swirl as he gently rolled the glass. *Finish this one and then stop.*

He took another swallow, holding the booze in his mouth for a moment before swallowing. Setting the glass down, he considered what he should do next. If he didn't do something, he'd finish off what was left in the bottle. From the sounds outside, the rain showed no immediate signs of letting up, but the thunder was softer, as if that part of the storm had moved off.

He loosened his tie and took off his jacket. Maybe he could find something to watch on TV. He'd sprung for the cable package with a full complement of sports channels; somebody was playing a basketball game out there tonight.

He pushed the glass away and opened the fridge, hoping he'd get lucky and find something he could nuke in the microwave oven. After pushing things around, Ian decided his best bet was to make a sandwich. Pulling out roast beef, cheddar cheese, and bread, he began to prepare his dinner.

Within a few minutes he flopped on the sofa and cranked up the TV, scrolling the channels till he found the Phoenix Suns. They were on the road and in Detroit, and the Pistons were in good form tonight. He liked the Suns, but truth be known, if the Celtics had been playing, it would have been a great night on the TV.

Jillian's answer earlier today had puzzled him a bit. Every guy who was into sports had a favorite team. Yet Wesley didn't. If Jillian was correct, then her brother was one weird guy.

***

Wes?" Jillian shouted as she entered the condo from the garage entrance. She stopped and waited for a few seconds, hoping for a reply.

"Meow!"

Simon padded from the hall and into the kitchen.

"That sounds like a complaint. Yes, I know. You haven't gotten near enough attention today."

She bent over and gently stroked the Siamese cat's back as he weaved his way around her hand and then her ankles. The contented purr vibrated beneath her touch and she scooped up her pet.

As Jillian traveled through the condo, she flipped on lamps and she surveyed the rooms. Everything, or what was left of her belongings, were back in their place.

Last night, after the police had left, she had spent three hours picking things up and putting them away. Now, she longed to turn on the TV or even the radio to fill the house with voices, noise, or some link to the outside world. Funny, she wasn't all that inclined to watch a lot of TV, but now that she didn't have it, she felt its absence. Should she go out and buy another one, or should she wait and see if the police would find anything?

She'd hoped and prayed that Sonoran Security would come through and find her brother, soon. Lord knows, it wasn't exactly inexpensive to hire them.

Jillian set down her cat, pulled the hair out of the pony tail, and went to change her clothes. Minutes later she stood in front of the refrigerator, inspecting the contents and trying to decide what she would have for dinner. In the end, she opened a can of vegetable soup and added a few crackers with cheese.

As she opened the can and poured the soup into a pot to warm, memories of her first one-on-one meeting with Ian this afternoon returned. She hadn't been too helpful. In fact, it was embarrassing that she couldn't provide much information on her brother's interests and hobbies. Was she really that out of touch?

No, she decided. Wesley had never been very talkative about things. Especially after he emerged from rehab. Whether he'd been embarrassed or it was his way of putting the events behind him, she didn't know.

When her parents had suggested he stay with her until he got back on his feet, Jillian had quickly agreed. But the man who had moved into her spare bedroom was a very different person from the younger brother from a few years back. He'd been quiet, almost to the point of secretive. In fact, the few times Jillian asked, all she got was the comment, "You're not my mother, quit acting like you are."

She was loath to admit it, but after a few weeks and several pushbacks from her brother, she retreated and stopped prying.

Jillian retrieved her cell phone from her purse and checked her voice mail and texts. Part of her feared a call back from the man who wanted money and the other part hoped that Wesley had surfaced to let her know he was safe.

Nothing.

She set the phone down and ladled soup into a bowl. She moved over to the small table in the corner of her kitchen, sat down, and ate her dinner. While she ate, she realized that she had not talked to either her parents or sister since the night before last and she owed them an update.

Jillian scrolled through the phone's contact book and selected her sister's number. She needed to talk to her sister first. Shelby had a knack for being able to get to the heart of things.

"Hello?"

"Hi, Shelby."

"Jillie, how's it going?"

"I've had better days."

"Oh boy, what happened?"

"Wesley hasn't checked in so I hired an agency to make an effort to find him."

"What?"

"After the police showed up, they pointed out the house hadn't actually been broken into. They asked who had a key and access. They suspect Wesley. I have the impression they're not going to put out an all-points bulletin to find him, so I took matters into my own hands."

"I thought that there was some sort of a waiting period before the police consider someone 'missing,'" Shelby said.

"Yes, you're correct. But he's in some sort of trouble," Jillian whispered. "I don't know the specifics but a man called today and said Wesley owes him fifty thousand dollars. He says that if Wes doesn't show up soon with the money, he wants me to pay this bill."

"What? Hold on a sec." Jillian heard her sister asked her husband to put the kids to bed. "Okay, I'm back. Who is this guy? Why does he believe Wes owes him fifty thousand?"

Jillian shook her head. "He says his name is Joe. Didn't provide a last name and I'm not even sure that is his real name. He hasn't provided any details behind why Wes would have borrowed a sum of money like that from him. But the man has information about me he shouldn't."

"What kind of information?"

"He said that I co-signed the loan, and if Wesley doesn't come up with the money soon, he expects me to pay the loan off."

Jillian leaned back in the chair and threaded her fingers through her hair as she swept it away from her face. "He knows my social security number, the Villa's annual revenue, and much more. I didn't agree to any loan, but I suspect that Wesley may have provided that information to him."

"Oh Jilli, I'm sorry." Then her sister went silent and seconds slowly stretched on, accentuating her sense of dread. Finally, Shelby asked, "Do you think he has started using drugs again?"

"I didn't see anything in his behavior that makes me believe that he is."

"Jilli, we didn't catch Wes's addiction until it was too late. I hope you're right."

Her sister's comment sounded innocent enough, and yet something about what her sister had said niggled at Jillian. "You sound as if you expected him to relapse."

"No I didn't expect him to, but kicking addiction is hard. Many people relapse."

There it is, the voice in her mind answered. The real reason for her sister's reservations.

"I hope I'm wrong. But we may have to face that possibility."

Jillian closed her eyes and recalled Matt had asked the same question this morning.

"So what is our next step?" Shelby asked.

"We have to wait and see what the agency finds out. I went to Sonoran Security. It's co-owned by Shawn Randall. Do you remember him from high school?"

"Not really. What do they think?"

"They haven't said much. We hope to learn more about the man who is calling about the money and hopefully we can work our way back to Wes."

Shelby exhaled. "It sounds like a reasonable place to start. I hope that they can get to the bottom of this quickly. Is there anything that I can do?"

"Can you hold off telling Mom and Dad about the phone calls and me hiring a detective agency for a day or so? Not until we have something to report. You know them. Mom will go crazy with worry and Dad will want to come out to Phoenix, and right now there's nothing we can do until we learn more to go on."

"Okay. But we'll have to tell them soon."

As a vision of her parents' faces flooded her mind, Jillian gulped. "Yeah, I know. Love you, sis."

"Love you too. Call me as soon as you hear something. Heck, call me tomorrow, even if you don't have anything more to report. Got it?"

"Yep."

Jillian ended the call and set the phone down on the small dinette table. Her hand traveled up to her lips and she gently rubbed them with her fingers. Her brother must be on the run.

Wesley, what have you gotten yourself into?

CHAPTER FIVE

Ian opened the door to the conference room. *Good.* He was the first one there, excluding Laura, who was in the process of setting up the bagels and coffee on the south end of a large mahogany table flanked by high backed leather chairs.

"Had breakfast?" Laura asked.

Ian grinned. "Just about to."

Laura laughed softly. "Help yourself." With that she exited the room. Ian set his Starbucks coffee down and headed over to the box of bagels and surveyed his choices.

"Dibs on the poppy seed one."

He glanced over at Paul, Thomas, and Sabrina as they entered the room. The trio, also dubbed from time to time as "The Three Musketeers" were Sonoran's tech team. Young and talented, they handled everything from background checks and research, to installation and support of security systems.

Thomas settled into a chair as Paul walked over and approached the food. "Sabrina, Laura got a jalapeno bagel. Do you want it?"

The petite raven-haired women looked up from the paperwork she was reviewing. She smiled and wrinkled her nose. "I really shouldn't. Too many carbs."

Paul rolled his eyes and grabbed the poppy seed bagel as if he thought the idea of continually dieting or watching carbs was a foolish idea. "Ian, if you want a jalapeno one, you better grab it before someone else does."

Ian grinned. "Thanks." He glanced over at Sabrina. "You sure?"

Sabrina nodded. "It's all yours."

He placed it on a small paper plate and began to add cream cheese.

Within a few minutes, Shawn entered, poured a coffee out of the carafe, and sat down. "Where's Matt?"

"He'll be here," Thomas replied. "He called and said that there was an accident and it bottle-necked traffic."

As if on cue, Matt cruised through the door. "Sorry I'm late."

He went to the end of the table and sat opposite Shawn. Ian noted that neither man sat at the head of the table. As Matt got situated, his brother studied the group. His eyes lighted on Ian and he felt his brother's scrutiny.

"Okay, let's get this meeting started," Matt said.

For the next few minutes, the tech team reviewed the projects on their schedule. Most of the discussion centered on clients scheduled to have alarms and/or security cameras added to their businesses. Ian wondered why he'd been asked to sit in on this meeting. Then he realized the reason when the topic Jillian and Wesley Connor came up for review.

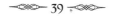

Paul spoke first. "We've done a background check and Jillian's story does check out. Wesley was arrested for cocaine possession and as part of the court judgement, he checked into rehab versus doing jail. Wesley never informed authorities who he got the drugs from though. It appears he's been clean since. His credit score is low. Looks like he's run up his credit cards close to the max."

Ian swallowed the mouthful of food and the bagel did a slow, uncomfortable decent to his stomach. He took a quick swallow from his coffee. "Do we have anything on the guy who called Jillian?"

The room went silent for a few moments. Ian feared that they had hit a wall when Thomas cleared his throat. The lanky, auburn-haired man looked at Matt, then Shawn, before squirming in his chair. "Okay, I have some intel, but we can't disclose how I got it. If anyone talks and this gets out, my source and I will be in major trouble. Got it?"

Ian looked from Thomas over to Shawn and Matt.

"Go ahead," Matt said.

"Okay, I have some friends who work for the mobile phone carriers. I made a few phone calls and have found out that his full name is Joseph Rossi."

Shawn shook his head. "Do we have anything else on him?"

"Yeah, we don't have his social security number, birthday and other data, so pulling a complete background check isn't possible. But, some preliminary searching on the internet and through the public court cases indicate he's been arrested for drug dealing around six years ago, but not arrested since."

"Do you think he's still dealing?" Matt asked.

"It's possible," Thomas said. "But it's also possible that he's moved up a bit and may be distributing and running dealers."

Thomas looked back to Matt. Sabrina continued to study the papers she had brought with her into the room, while Paul stared so intently at his bagel that Ian wondered if he was trying to count the number of poppy seeds on it.

"I don't get it," Ian responded. "When he called Jillian yesterday, he told her that Wesley owed him fifty thousand dollars. He knew stuff about Wesley and Jillian that he shouldn't. Things like their social security numbers, personal and business tax info. Drug dealing is a cash business. How does that fit in?"

No one answered. Ian looked from one person to another, hoping one of the team would come up with an answer that would explain this.

Ian continued. "The conversation with Rossi totally blindsided Jillian. She keeps insisting that Wesley isn't using drugs."

"How in the world did Wesley Connors connect with Rossi?" Matt asked.

"It wouldn't be as far-fetched as you think," Sabrina replied as she looked up from her papers. "Consider this. Wesley could have a drug problem, and ends up running drugs for Rossi. Let's face it, an outside sales job would position you well for making the rounds at clubs and bars. Those are certainly venues where drugs could be sold and consumed."

"So you're proposing Wesley Connors is a drug dealer and possibly an addict?"

"I'm not saying that he is, but if you want a working theory as to how they know each other, this one should be considered," Sabrina said calmly.

Matt glanced over at Ian with a grim expression. "All right, if we start with this theory, where would we look for him?"

The three young employees looked at each other. "Well, if he's doing drugs and has 'crashed', then we should search for him in places where he can hide out and people will ask few questions."

"Such as?" Ian asked.

"I'd start with the obvious," Paul said. "Hotels where they take cash. It's unlikely you'll find him at the local Marriott; they'll want a credit card on file. We're talking dumps, like the stuff you find on Van Buren or some of the rundown areas of downtown Mesa."

"Also, I don't know how hard the police are searching. But if we can get serial numbers on the electronics, we could hit pawn shops in that area. Maybe he's pawned stuff."

Shawn leaned back in his chair and pushed the remains of his bagel away. "This is going to be ugly. I can sense it. Refresh my memory. Did Jillian provide the make, model and license plate for his car?"

"Yes, we have that," Sabrina replied.

"Okay, today, since we're caught up on other projects, we'll put you three on making the rounds through the motels. Look for his car, be discreet, if you have to grease a palm or two, do it," Shawn said.

"Sabrina. I want you to start hitting the pawn shops. See if you can find anything," Matt added.

Sabrina's gaze narrowed. "I can help with the hotel search. I'm the only one here fluent in Spanish. That may be useful."

"I know. But the places they're going are rough. Pimps, hookers, drug addicts." He raised his hand to stop her commenting. "Besides, your communication skills will also be highly useful as you work the pawn shops too."

Sabrina pressed her lips together, but nodded. "Okay. Fine. If you insist. I'm on it."

"All right, meeting adjourned," Shawn said.

As the group arose from their chairs, Shawn spoke quietly. "Ian, can you please stay for a couple seconds?"

Ian sank back down in his chair and watched as everyone left without a comment. He studied each of them, looking for a hint or clue as to what they thought, but he couldn't discern anything.

Thomas closed the door behind him as he exited.

"When you leave, go back to Jillian Connor's business. If Rossi can't find her brother, he's likely to come down hard on Jillian."

"Agreed. I don't know how forthcoming she will be. Yesterday was awkward. My questions not only irritated her, I think it caused her to shut me down."

"You'll need to be a diplomat. Know when to push and when to back off."

"Easier said than done," Ian said. He rose from his chair.

"One more thing," Shawn added.

Ian stopped. His brother reached into his shirt pocket and held out what looked to be a business card.

"What's this?"

"Someone I think you need to have a talk with."

Ian took the card and read it. *Therapist, counselor? No way.* Ian dropped the card to the table and slid it back to his brother. "You think I'm crazy?"

"No. I think hurting is a better word. Look, only you know what happened, what you saw or did. But I can tell you this. Whatever it is, it's eating you alive."

Shawn stopped talking and locked eyes with him. Worry

graced his brother's eyes. "This guy works with returning soldiers. I think he can help. Consider it."

Ian swallowed. Was it so bad that his brother was scared that he'd lose it? Shawn stood up and gathered his things.

"Morgan wants to have you over for dinner."

Great. Tell me I'm going crazy and then invite me to have dinner with your girlfriend. Give me a glimpse of normal. Something I don't have and you don't think I'm capable of.

"I'll tell her you're currently on a case, but as soon as things are wrapped up, we come up with a firm date."

"Okay," Ian said quietly.

His brother exited the room and closed the door behind him. Ian stood in silence as he waited for his brother to walk away from the room. Irritation washed out and weariness settled in. Did they think he was a risk? Should he quit?

"No," Ian whispered.

He picked up the card and looked for the nearest trashcan. Then he stopped and looked at the card again. *Maybe later.* He stuffed the card into his jacket pocket and picked up his stuff. He had a job to do.

***

Jillian made a beeline for the lunchroom and the coffeemaker. *Seven-thirty.* A good sixty to ninety minutes earlier than her normal arrival time and she was already exhausted.

Last night's conversation with Shelby hadn't gone as Jillian had expected. She had sought her sister's comfort, understanding, and support. Instead, questions had been raised on whether her brother had started using drugs again. Jillian had spent the majority of the night tossing and turning, replaying her time with Wesley since he moved in and tried to pick up the pieces of his life. Was her sister correct? Had she missed something?

Heck, even Ian's questions yesterday had brought that unnerving suspicion to light. Jillian felt like an idiot. He thought she was clueless, or worse, hiding something from him.

As she popped the K-cup into the Keurig, while the coffee brewed, she considered what needed to be done. Today the wedding set-up would go into high gear. This bride had elected to have the wedding ceremony at the La Villa as well as the reception. So while the dining room had been set yesterday, today the small chapel would be prepped. Flowers, candles, and a crucifix would be set up and later this afternoon the wedding party would arrive for a run-through. Today promised to be an action-packed day.

The coffee maker stopped. She removed her cup, adding creamer and sugar. One thing she knew for sure, Ian would be back as well and have more questions. She raised the mug to her face and inhaled the rich smell before taking a sip. Whether she liked it or not, it was time to get some facts and face what she was up against.

She walked back to her office and sank into the chair. Her cell phone rang. Jillian looked at the number. She picked up the call. "Hi, Ian."

"I've just come out of the meeting where the team has updated us on things. I need some information. Do you have a minute or two?"

Oh boy, here it comes. She sucked a breath, and then answered, "Yes, go ahead."

"Do you have any serial numbers on the electronics that are missing?"

"Some of them. I submitted what information I had to the police yesterday morning. I have a copy of what I sent over to them." She pulled paperwork out of her large tote bag.

"I'm ready to take the information down when you're ready."

The next few minutes Jillian gave descriptions and read off the numbers, which she'd retrieved after the police left. When she finished, she asked, "Anything more?"

"Yes. Does Wes have access to your business accounts and do you have the ability to look at his bank balances?"

"No. But he uses the same investment advisor that I have. He inherited money from my grandmother as well. I can make a phone call. Maybe the financial advisor will share some information with me."

"Call them. Let me know what you find out," Ian said.

"Okay."

"I'm on my way in. I want to talk more when I get there."

Jillian pressed her lips together tightly. Seconds passed.

"Jillian, are you there?"

"Yes," she said quietly. "I'll be here when you arrive."

***

Ian set the phone down, grabbed the plate with the half-eaten bagel and tossed it into the trashcan. The fact that Wesley had disappeared, taking expensive electronics, fit the theory that he was using drugs again. He took a deep breath, stood up, and headed to his brother's office. The door sat open and his brother was reviewing some papers. He knocked on the door.

His brother glanced over to him in the doorway with wary eyes. He probably expected Ian to follow up with their earlier conversation.

"I've got the serial numbers, and Jillian is checking with her financial advisor to find out about Wesley's inheritance."

"Oh?" Shawn leaned back in his chair and exhaled.

"Jillian's grandmother left substantial funds to the grandchildren. Jillian is checking to see if Wesley has touched his. I should know more when I meet with her later."

Shawn nodded and pointed to the paper in Ian's hand. "Is that the list?"

"Yeah." Ian moved forward to the desk and handed it to his brother.

Shawn scanned the list. "I'll get this to the tech team. You'd better head over to La Villa de Gardenia."

"On my way," Ian replied. As he walked to the door, he sensed his brother watch him leave. He straightened and walked out the door, refusing to look back and meet his gaze. This was no time to get distracted by his brother's concern about if he could handle this case.

CHAPTER SIX

An hour later, Ian stood at the door of Jillian's office. She sat behind her desk with a puzzled look and was absentmindedly toying with the end of her ponytail.

"Hi."

She glanced over, flashed a forced smile, and dropped her hand from her hair. "Come in. Have a seat." She gestured at the leather chair in front of her desk. "I've checked with our financial advisor. Found out some more information."

"Good or bad."

"Bad. I spoke to John, our advisor. He said that Wesley closed out his accounts and moved his money a couple months ago. Wesley inherited the same amount of money from our grandmother as I did. That would have been two hundred and fifty thousand dollars. The insurance company paid for most of his rehab. Ian, I had no idea he did this. John reported that he didn't roll over the money to another advisor or fund. Wesley just withdrew it. Somewhere near two hundred and fifty thousand has disappeared."

Ian cleared his throat. "Actually, if Rossi is correct, it might be more like three hundred thousand."

Jillian sank back in her office chair and rubbed her eyes. "Right. Let's not forget that we've got a stranger claiming that Wesley owes him money too. What's another fifty thousand at this point?"

"We've got a theory as to what's going on."

Jillian looked at him. "What have you got?"

"A little information on Rossi. He was arrested a number of years ago for dealing drugs. We think he may still be involved in that line of business, but may have moved up the food chain and is now running some dealers." Ian took a slow breath. "I'm sorry that I have to ask this, but would Wesley deal drugs?

Jillian stared at him in silence. "Let me get this straight, yesterday my brother was a relapsed drug addict and today the working theory is that he is a dealer too?"

Ian leaned back. "Jillian, Wesley's job put him in frequent contact with clubs, restaurants, casinos and bars. It would be an excellent job to have if you needed to deal or distribute this stuff."

"No." Jillian replied. She studied Ian. For crying out loud, he knew her younger brother and knew how hard he had worked to come clean. "No, absolutely no way. He isn't a drug dealer."

"Are you sure? I mean, a relapse might happen even under the most innocent of circumstances. It can be a pretty slippery slope from there."

Jillian brought up her hand and rubbed her forehead. She'd

attended some classes while her brother was in recovery and had become familiar with the theory of addictive personality disorder.

"You think that I wouldn't know. You're wrong. I would. Wes was not doing drugs. Granted, I can't explain the disappearance of his inheritance, and I don't know how or why Rossi figures into this, but…"

She paused as she chewed on the idea that perhaps she'd missed something. "Did I do the right thing to let Wes move in while he got on his feet?" Jillian asked.

Ian didn't answer immediately. "You know, sometimes you do what you believe is in someone's best interest. It comes from a place of love and your heart and mind are convinced it's the correct thing. It never occurs to you that there could be a dark side to it."

Dark side. The words stood out as they'd been shouted. Jillian wondered if he was referring to more than just what happened with her brother.

Part of her wanted to ask questions, delve deeper. But Ian Randall's personal history wasn't her business. Not anymore. Besides, once this mystery was solved, he'd move on, probably relieved to be out of her messy life.

"So what do we do next?"

"Well," Ian replied. "Our tech teams are becoming street teams as we speak. They are checking out the hotels. Places where the owners are happy to take cash and ask few if any questions. We're also checking out the pawn shops to see if we can locate any of the missing items. It's possible that if Wesley was in urgent need of money, he sold them for quick cash."

"Okay," Jillian replied. "I would go help look, but I'm stuck here. Tomorrow is the wedding. That means that food is being delivered today, the cooks will be doing some prep, the chapel will be decorated, flowers will be arriving, wait staff will be checking in and picking up their uniforms, and they are having a run-through of the actual ceremony before the families take off for the rehearsal dinner."

"Is your facility hosting the rehearsal dinner?"

"No. The ceremony walkthrough is scheduled for three-thirty. Usually they don't take too long." Jillian began to assemble the papers on her desk. "In fact, I need to go out and meet with the crew to get the chapel set-up started."

Ian cracked a gentle smile. "You might want to stop by the ladies room and freshen up a bit."

Jillian looked at him and then began to look at her dress. "Why? What's wrong?"

"Um, you smudged your eye makeup when you rubbed your eyes."

Her hands flew to her face.

"Oh, great." She sighed, and then grabbed her purse. "Thanks for telling me. I'll be back shortly. What are you going to do today?"

"Be around you. We don't know exactly what is going on with Joe Rossi, but if he is correct and Wesley owes him fifty thou, you haven't heard the last from him, and when he surfaces I want to be there."

Heat flushed her face and she glanced away. Something in his answer made her feel safe, secure, and as if things would turn out well. "Um, I'll be back in a few minutes."

***

Jillian strode down the shaded hallway that circled the open courtyard.

"There." She gestured to the metal door, which had been painted a dark brown to match, at least on the surface, the wooden ones which led to the meeting room. Ian lengthened his stride reaching the door seconds before her and opening it wide.

"Thanks," she murmured as she gave him a smile. The scent of a light floral perfume wafted through the air as she passed him. She turned and waited for him as he followed her through the entrance.

"So this is where all the culinary magic takes place."

"Absolutely." A short stocky man who wore a white chef's jacket looked up from the meat that he was inspecting.

He looked over at Jillian. "Wondered when you would show up."

She gestured to the man. "Ian, this is Larry, our head chef."

Ian took a couple of steps and extended his hand. "Nice to meet you."

"How's it going?" Jillian asked.

"Looks good. The steaks have just arrived, the vegetables are in the walk-in fridge, and the liquor should be here soon. Marie will be here in an hour or so to bake and put together the wedding cake. The team is ready to be here early tomorrow to prep and cook for the reception. We're set."

"You said the liquor is arriving this afternoon?" Ian asked.

"Yes, we always bring it in the day before." Larry looked over at his boss for verification.

Jillian frowned. "Ian, is anything wrong?"

"I'm assuming that your vendor is your brother's company, right?"

"Yes.

"Okay, bear with me because I'm still trying to get a handle on things. But when was the order placed for this reception?"

"I get what you're thinking. But this order was placed weeks ago when the event was booked, the deposit was made and the menu for the reception was set."

Ian raked his hand through his hair and then sighed. "Just a thought."

"Not a bad one."

Ian glanced over at Larry, who seemed to not catch the subtext of their conversation. Apparently, Jillian had kept the recent developments from her employees.

"I've got more stuff to finish checking. Do you have anything else?" The chef trained his gaze on Jillian and waited as if he expected that there may be more questions.

"No. That's good. Thanks."

Larry returned to finish checking in the shipment. After they exited the kitchen, Ian commented. "I take it none of your employees know what's happened."

She gazed at him, pressed her lips together, and slowly inhaled.

"No," she replied in a quiet voice. "I haven't shared that information. Not yet. With all that is going on tomorrow, I need my team focused on providing the best service possible and not whispering in bathrooms about what happened."

"That's wise."

Jillian closed her eyes briefly, and Ian swore he could see exhaustion settle on her like a cloak. She sighed. "The rehearsal should start soon. If the wedding planner is half as good as I think she is, the wedding party will be in and out of here fairly quickly. Is there anything I need to do?"

Ian paused. He sensed that having to wait patiently without any information was eating her up inside, and frankly right now he had nothing. He hated disappointing her and felt that if they made some little progress, both of them would feel better.

"I have an idea."

Jillian's eyes opened and a sudden gleam flashed in them. "What?"

"You mentioned that your brother's employer told you that Wes had requested a couple days off."

"Yeah."

"Well, those two days are past. What if we leave after the rehearsal and pay his manager a face-to-face visit and see if Wes has called in, or reported in."

"You think he knows something?"

"Don't know, but let's find out."

"Okay."

As if on cue, people threaded through the entrance and began to assemble. Ian surveyed the growing crowd. The bride and her bridesmaids weren't hard to miss. They chatted, laughed, and circled around a small brunette woman as if the world would stop if they ignored her. He peeked at Jillian and she watched them with a detached expression. Then her gaze traveled to the entrance as the woman who Ian had seen here yesterday walked through the wrought iron gate and into the courtyard.

"Wedding planner, twelve o'clock," he muttered.

Jillian laughed softly and glanced back at him. "This will be over soon, I promise."

She was true to her word. The whole walk-through took less than forty minutes. Ian had to give it to the wedding planner. She knew when to push to get things moving forward, albeit politely, and when to back off and let the families socialize. He'd assumed that Jillian would be involved, but both she and Ian stayed in the back of the chapel and waited, ready to swing into action if there was a last minute request for a change.

After the party left, Ian escorted Jillian as she made the rounds, double checked doors, and ensured that they were all locked. Ian stood at the entrance of the chapel and surveyed the courtyard. The kitchen lights were still on.

"Marie will be here for a few more hours baking, decorating, and assembling the wedding cake." Jillian commented. "She'll lock up the kitchen and re-lock the front gate when she leaves."

She paused. "Let me go to the office and collect my stuff. I'll be back in a couple of minutes."

Ian nodded. "Take your time."

He watched her walk away from him. Her brisk pace from earlier had become a slower and more seductive cadence, in Ian's opinion. She paused and then glanced back at him. The corners of her lips turned up gently. *Oh you flirt. You knew I'd watch you.* He crooked a grin at her and tapped his watch.

"Okay," she mouthed before heading back to her office.

Had he made a mistake suggesting that they visit Wesley's place of employment? Despite her playfulness a few seconds ago, she was also looking tired. The adrenaline that she had been running on the past couple of days was washing out and exhaustion would probably provide her with the first full night of sleep in two days.

Minutes ticked by as Ian strolled over to the fountain and watched the water cascade down an ornately carved fountain that looked to be at least ten feet tall.

"Ready?"

Ian turned. "Do you want me to drive?"

"Okay. We can swing by and pick up my car after we come back. Are you parked out front?"

"Yeah."

They headed for the entrance to La Villa de Gardena. He fished for his keys and pushed open the gate to the courtyard entrance as Jillian walked through. Ian caught a whiff of light floral perfume as she slid by him. As she turned and locked the gate, he noted that she'd also applied some lip color. For a second, déjà vu hit and he felt like they were on a date. Lord, how long had it been since he'd been on a proper date? Months? *Longer than that*, the voice in his head responded. *And you need to get a social life*, the voice in his head added.

Ian cleared his throat and pointed to his Toyota Corolla. "Your chariot awaits."

Jillian chuckled and he mentally checked himself. Had he really said that? Geez, that was seriously a corny remark. He glanced over at her and noticed she had trained her gaze to the ground as they walked toward his vehicle. He tamped down the impulse to reach out and touch her. Make contact and perhaps find out what she was thinking about. Instead, he punched the button on the key fob and the Corolla's doors unlocked. Ian made the conscious choice to not open the door for her. He needed a few seconds of distance from her before he got into the vehicle. She slid into the passenger seat with no comment and buckled the seat belt.

Jillian provided brief instructions on how to get to Wesley's employer before settling back into the seat. The silence in the car interior lingered, and Ian toyed with the idea of turning on the radio, or pursuing further questioning. He reached for the console to turn on the radio when she spoke. "Why do you believe Wesley has relapsed and is using again?"

Ian returned his hand to the steering wheel and cast a quick glance over to her. Jillian stared out the side window and watched the scenery roll by. His first impression was that she was relaxed, but the soft tapping of fingers on her lap gave her away.

He cleared his throat and swallowed as he considered how to tell her what he knew would probably break her heart. He didn't want to hurt Jillian, but if things turned out badly for her brother, she needed to be prepared. To lead her to believe everything would come out fine would be lying to her and more hurtful in the long run.

"Two reasons. First, addicts often sell possessions to raise funds for their habits. Second, a man who has a criminal record as a drug dealer is looking for him."

Jillian remained silent. The tension coiled and then stretched as the seconds ticked on. Ian looked over and she continued to stare out the passenger side window. He touched her arm. She didn't pull back, or even look at him for pity's sake. "Hey."

"As much as I don't want to believe it, you could be right."

The flat resignation in her voice clawed at his gut. She was hurt and there was little he could do about it.

Twenty minutes later, Ian pulled the car into a visitor parking space at Cactus Distributing. "What is the name of Wes's manager?"

"Steven Nelson."

"Do you think he'll see us?"

Jillian nodded and pointed to a man in dress slacks and a white shirt with rolled up sleeves who was walking over to the covered parking space. "That's him. Come on."

With that comment she opened the door and slid out, leaving her purse behind. She began to walk briskly to the man. Ian exited the car and locked it, following a few steps behind.

"Mr. Nelson!" Jillian shouted.

The heavy-set man stopped, turned, and studied her as she approached him. "I'm Jillian Connors, Wesley's sister. Could I have a few minutes of your time to chat?"

The man's face crumpled into a frown. "I shouldn't be talking with you. If you have any questions, you should talk with your brother."

The manager's eyes swept the parking lot nervously, lighting on Ian. Ian stopped and waited as Jillian continued to approach Nelson. "I would love to have a conversation with my brother, but he's missing."

She stopped, leaving a few feet between them. Ian studied the man's body language. He slowly rocked, placing his weight on one foot and then the other as he scanned the parking lot to see if anyone else was around. Steve Nelson was on edge. Ian had spent enough time in war zones long enough to recognize that emotion a mile away.

"I need some information and your help."

Her voice carried in the nearly empty parking lot. She wasn't exactly pleading, more like commanding his help.

Nelson cleared his throat. "I'm sorry this happened. But I had no choice."

Jillian threw a glance over to Ian and then returned her attention to Wesley's manager. "What happened?"

Nelson, opened his mouth to talk and then stopped and watched Ian approach. "Look, I was just doing my job."

"Of course," Jillian replied. "What happened?

Ian walked up and stopped next to Jillian. Wesley's manger's face was flushed and sweat beaded on his brow and upper lip as he clutched his suit jacket tightly. Almost as if Ian had shouted "boo" he'd scamper away like a scared rabbit.

"Mr. Nelson, I'm Ian Randall and our agency has been hired to help Ms. Connors locate Wesley. Any information you can provide to help us would be greatly appreciated."

The manager nodded and looked down at the asphalt. He was weighing the variables. Ian had no doubt that if he could look inside Nelson's brain, he'd see the gears turning quickly.

"Mr. Nelson, I think Wesley's in some kind of trouble," Jillian said.

His head snapped up and he eyed her. Then, whatever the issue had been that the man had been mulling over, the decision had been made. "I don't know about that, but I can tell you that I let your brother go today."

Jillian paled and her voice came out softly. "Today? Why?"

Nelson sighed. "A couple of reasons. It had been building for a long time."

"And those reasons were?" Ian asked.

"He hadn't been meeting his sales quota. In fact, he missed them for the last four months. Wesley had been placed on performance improvement. I would have bet money he'd turn it around."

The manager glanced over to Jillian. "Your brother was a great salesman, a natural. But, he didn't make his goals this month. In fact, in the last couple weeks, he stopped showing up regularly to the office. After not responding to phone calls or emails, and when he didn't return from his requested days off, we had to let him go for job abandonment."

"I didn't know that. He never said anything," she whispered.

"I'm sorry," Nelson replied. "Like I said, I had to do my job."

Jillian nodded, her face pale. She opened her mouth as if she was going to say something and then closed it. Ian stepped over and gently took her arm. "Thank you for your assistance, Mr. Nelson."

"Yeah," the manager replied. With that, he continued on to his car.

"What do we do now?" Jillian asked.

She looked up at Ian as he escorted her back to his car. Tears clung to her lashes. He took a deep breath. "Jillian, I need you to think. Does he have any close friends he may go to?"

Jillian walked stiffly as if her legs had turned to wood and stared into the distance as she considered his question. "Maybe Roger," she murmured. "He and Wes were high school friends and kept in touch over the years; perhaps he knows something."

"All right. Let's go," Ian said. He gently began to guide her back to his Toyota.

She walked slowly, "We need to see Roger. Tonight."

"Agreed. Do you know where he lives?"

"Yes." Jillian began to walk more briskly to the car.

Ian unlocked the doors and watched her open the door and get in. Ian hung back and hissed a curse under his breath. They needed to find her brother and fast, or this would not end well.

CHAPTER SEVEN

"Is Roger home?"

With obvious caution, the young woman stared back through the screened front porch at Jillian. Her gaze lingered on Jillian for a few seconds before focusing on Ian.

"I'm Wesley Connors' sister. He's missing, and I'm hoping you might help me find him," Jillian added.

The last three words appeared to penetrate the haze of her thoughts and the woman unlocked the door. "Come in."

Ian followed Jillian into the house. The front living room was small, typical of houses built in the sixties. The inside was neat, clean, and furnished simply. An overstuffed dark brown leather sofa dominated the room, opposite of a TV stand where a large flat screen TV sat.

The young woman gestured for Jillian and Ian to sit. "I'm Ashley, Roger's fiancée. Can I get you something to drink? Water, iced tea?"

"No thank you," Jillian replied.

Ian studied Ashley. The woman was slender and her blonde hair had been flat-ironed so that it fell to just beyond her shoulders. She wore faded jeans and a tight t-shirt. What struck him as odd was how calm she was. If someone had shown up at his doorstep and announced his fiancée's best friend had gone missing, he'd be more concerned.

"I came home from work two nights ago and I found our house had been ransacked. Wesley didn't respond to my calls or texts and hasn't show up since."

Ashley swallowed and her eyes traveled from Jillian over to him. *Curious. She's curious about me.* Her expression hardened into suspicion. She asked Ian, "Who are you?"

"My name is Ian Randall. I work for Sonoran Security and Jillian has retained the company to assist in locating her brother."

Ashley's eyes widened slightly before returning to normal. "I don't know where he is," she whispered.

"Do you know what happened?" Jillian asked.

Ashley shook her head. "No."

Jillian continued. "The police have pointed out that there was no forced entry. They probably believe Wes took them, and we're concerned that maybe Wesley has relapsed and started using drugs again." Jillian paused, swept her hair back with a trembling hand, and then straightened.

For the first time since they met, Ian perceived a break in the other woman's reserve. "No I don't believe that. I never saw anything in his behavior that would lead me to believe that he was using again."

Ashley grasped the top of Jillian's hand that lay tightened into a fist on her lap. Jillian glanced over at Ian and a relieved, soft smile bloomed on her face before returning her gaze back at the woman. "I'm glad to hear that. It just doesn't look good."

Ian said nothing. Now someone else had reinforced Jillian's belief by saying Wesley wasn't using drugs. If Ashley meant to help, it most likely would backfire when Jillian ultimately would have to face the facts.

"Jillian, Wes is a good guy and would have never have done something like this unless there was a good reason," Ashley said. Her voice held an earnestness to it that was compelling.

"Ashley." The moment the word came from his lips, both women looked up at him. "We've just discovered that Wesley has lost his job. There has been a deterioration of his performance, unexplained absences, and they finally terminated him. We need your help. Can you give us any information as to what happened or where we can find him?"

The woman shook her head. "He said nothing when he visited Monday evening to watch football with Roger. No, wait." Ashley froze and stared off to the other side of the room, as if she was recalling those memories and playing them back in her mind. "Oh my."

"What?" Ian asked.

Her hands moved up to her lips. "He was really upset when the Detroit Pistons lost. He left shortly before the game ended. In fact, he practically bolted out of here. He just said he had to go. It was kind of weird."

Ian frowned and looked at Jillian.

"Ashley, we would like to contact Wesley's other friends, and we don't have any contact info. Do you have some names and phone numbers so we could check in with them?" Jillian asked.

The woman shook her head. "I'm afraid I can't be of much help. Roger would know. He's still at work right now. When Wesley came over, it wasn't uncommon to see the two of them outside at the barbecue having a beer and chatting while they cooked the steaks. Occasionally, a bunch of the guys would go to the casinos or a sports bar, watch a game or two, and have a few beers. You know, a 'boys night out'. That kind of stuff. Maybe he told Roger things."

"When will Roger be home?"

The woman glanced at her watch. "Not for another couple of hours. His employer lets him come in later in the morning and he stays until well after six before he leaves the office. Helps to miss the rush hour traffic."

"Okay," Ian replied. "Here is my business card and when Roger gets home please have him give me a call."

"Wait." Jillian extended her hand to Ashley. "Let me put my cell number on it."

The young woman handed the card over and Jillian pulled out a pen and added her phone number before returning it.

"Have Roger give me a call," Jillian said. "We're trying to solve this puzzle and anything, even the smallest scrap of information, could be useful."

"Of course," Ashley replied.

The young woman glanced down at his card and then looked at Jillian. "I'll have him call, even if he has nothing to report."

Jillian smiled and slowly rose from the sofa. "Thanks."

Ian took his cue and stood up, and within a couple of minutes they were back in his vehicle. Jillian sank into the seat on the passenger side and Ian turned on the ignition.

"What do you think?" Jillian asked.

Ian threw her a quick look before turning his gaze back to the traffic. "Not sure. I thought her response when you told her Wes was missing was strange. I mean, she didn't appear shocked. It wasn't until after you mentioned that the police suspect he stole the stuff at your house that she opened up and I saw some emotion. I don't know. Did you think she seemed surprised?"

"No," Jillian replied. "But I was afraid if I had forced the issue, she would've shut down and we'd have gotten nothing from her."

Ian nodded. He was a bit relieved that Jillian had come to the same conclusion.

She leaned back in the seat. "What now?"

Ian glanced over at her as he fastened his seat belt. Jillian had crossed her legs. The right leg rested on top and it rocked back and forth. He tamped down the urge to touch her and soothe away the nervous energy which bubbled to the surface.

"I'm going to check in with the office to let them know what we've discovered and find out if they've been successful in uncovering some information. In the meantime, I'm taking you back to your car and I want you to go home. You're exhausted and need a good night's sleep."

Jillian snorted a small, soft laugh. "I'd love that. I haven't slept well since this all started. My mind keeps working on it, chewing on every angle, hoping that there is something that I didn't miss."

Ian felt for her. Insomnia…. He had that mastered. Not that sleeping was any escape. His memories wormed their way into his dreams, twisting into nightmares.

"You've been running on adrenaline the past couple days, and I think you'll have no problems tonight."

"Hope you're right."

Her cell phone went off. Jillian fished it out of her purse and looked at the number. "Oh boy."

"What?"

"It's Rossi."

"Give me your phone." Ian, in a matter of seconds, had picked up the call and placed the speaker phone on before handing it back to Jillian.

"Hello?" Jillian said.

"Have you located your brother?"

Ian's hands tightened on the steering wheel. Joe Rossi didn't waste time on cordial greetings. His tone was brusque and no-nonsense. Jillian paused and tapped Ian on the arm, "What do I say?" she mouthed.

"Tell him the truth," Ian silently responded.

"Uh, Mr. Rossi, we've started to make some inquiries. Wesley was terminated from his job earlier this week, and I've met with his best friend's fiancé. She reported that he was there to watch football on Monday night. She didn't know anything about his disappearance."

Silence followed Jillian's response. Finally, the caller spoke. "Well, I'll give you a couple more days to find him. But if you can't, I will expect you to pay off his loan."

Jillian croaked out, "The fifty thousand dollar loan?"

"That's the one," Rossi answered in a flat, low voice that almost resembled a growl.

"What if I can't?"

"You and I both know you can. All it will take is some movement of funds or liquidation of assets and you can make me go away."

Jillian glanced over at Ian. The pleading look in her face left no room for doubt that she was at a loss for how to respond.

"Ms. Connors, please let the tall gentleman who is driving you know that refusal to take care of this obligation will have consequences."

"Such as?" Ian blurted out the question, and then immediately wished he could punch a reset button. Even to his ears, he sounded belligerent, and taunting a man like Rossi was a foolish thing to do.

"Come, come Mr. Randall. That is your name, isn't it? Counseling your client to ignore their obligation isn't a good idea. Failure brings consequences."

Ian was speechless. How did this man know who he was? He'd not seen that coming. He sucked in a breath of air. "If you know who I am, then you know who I work for. Threatening a client, especially in front of another person, isn't a wise thing to do."

Ian let the verbal counter punch hang in the air. Then he heard it. It sounded like the man had laughed. "Okay, I see talking with you isn't going anywhere. But, Mr. Randall, don't doubt what I said. You will know that soon."

A chill washed through Ian. He glanced over at Jillian, who stared at the phone in her hand with a pinched expression on her face.

"Two more days," Rossi stated. Then the phone call disconnected.

Jillian's hand dropped to her lap.

"We know one thing," Ian stated.

"Oh?"

"Your brother is on the run from Rossi."

The couple sat in silence for the next few minutes as Ian drove back to La Villa de Gardenia. By now the sun had settled low on the horizon, and dusk was rapidly becoming night. He turned on the Corolla's lights and drove across the parking lot toward Jillian's BMW.

Jillian gasped as he stopped his car. The car's headlights flooded her car in bright light. Crumpled glass littered the pavement and the hood of the car, while someone, not happy with just bashing the windows, had taken a knife and slashed the tires.

As he stopped the car, Jillian scrambled out of it and walked around the car, surveying the damage. She stopped in front of the driver's side and crossed her arms before her right hand traveled up to her lips and pressed against them.

Rossi's words floated in his mind. *I mean business and you will know that soon.*

***

"Come on Shawn, pick up." Ian muttered the words as he listened to the phone ring. Forget waiting for the morning meeting. He needed to check in now and get some instructions as to what to do next.

He looked over at Jillian on the phone with the police. She'd have to call the towing company next to haul her vehicle into the dealership.

"Ian, what's up?"

He spun on a heel and took a few steps away from Jillian. "We've got some issues here. Things have escalated."

"Fill me in."

His brother's voice was calm and vaguely reminded him of an officer asking for a status report. Ian took the next few minutes updating his brother about the information they discovered earlier and finished with a full mechanical assessment of the damage to Jillian's car.

"Has the tech team found out anything?" Ian asked.

"Not yet. They had nothing when they reported in a couple hours ago. But if Wesley's best friend's fiancé had told the truth, then it's likely that Wesley is on the run from Rossi and the challenge of finding him just grew exponentially."

Ian cast a quick look over at Jillian and noted that she was still on the phone to the police.

"Hey, I can certainly drive Jillian back to her house, but I don't think that's a good idea. Rossi knows way too much about her. Heck, he even knew who I was. The joker addressed me by my name."

Ian paced back and forth on the asphalt waiting for his brother to reply. He was about to speak when Shawn chimed in. "You're right, the hotels aren't secure, but we don't have a safe house."

"What do you recommend?" Ian asked.

"You have your pistol at your apartment, right?"

Oh great. Based on Shawn's question, he could see where this was going and the last thing he wanted was a client bunking down on his sofa. Not like his place was a dump or anything. More like your basic, never-got-around-to-decorating bachelor pad.

He sighed. "So you're telling me to take Jillian to her home, have her pack her bags, and then bring her back to my place."

"That's probably the best option right now."

"Bro, if we're going to take these types of cases on in the future, we need to figure out the 'safe house' issue."

Shawn laughed. "You're right. We do."

"All right. I'll check in in the morning. Unless something else pops up."

He disconnected and walked back to Jillian.

"The police will be here shortly. I'm pretty sure this won't take long. They'll probably just write up another report, like they did two days ago when I reported the robbery." Jillian said.

"How are you doing?"

The sides of her mouth turned up into a weary smile. "I've had better days." She glanced over at the entrance. "The lights are still on. Marie's still here."

Jillian's eyes widened. "You don't think that they..." She didn't complete the sentence but turned and began to jog to the front gate.

Ian sprinted and caught up with her. "Jillian, wait."

She arrived at the door, grasped the gate and yanked hard. It swung open, throwing her off balance, and she staggered back. "Ian, I locked this when I left. Marie has a key, but given she's inside by herself, she would have locked the gate behind her." She studied the lock. "It looks okay."

"Stay here." Ian swept past her into the courtyard and scanned the facilities. There didn't appear to be any vandalism and the place was empty. He turned left and marched down the covered walkway down to the kitchen. As he got closer he heard country music. Apparently the cook turned up the music when she was pulling a late night wedding cake baking session. He peered through the small window into the kitchen and spied the woman assembling tiers of cakes on a platter.

He knocked on the door, and the poor woman nearly jumped

out of her skin. Something touched his shoulder, and he whirled around. Jillian staggered back a couple steps, nearly falling.

He grasped her arms and steadied her. "I told you to wait."

"Marie is my employee." She stepped up to the window and looked inside. Within seconds, the door was unlocked and opened.

"You two nearly scared me to death," Marie exclaimed as she opened the door.

"Sorry. We didn't mean to. Someone vandalized my car and we're checking to see if you are okay," Jillian replied.

"Yeah, I'm fine. You know me. I always crank up the radio when I work on decorating the cakes. Even if a bomb had gone off, I probably wouldn't have heard it."

Ian smirked. He'd heard the 'I wouldn't have heard a bomb' comment one too many times from people who had no concept as to how loud one of those monsters could be.

"We've called the police. After we file a report, Ian will give me a ride home. Did you see or hear anything?"

Marie turned down the volume on the radio, which resided on the counter next to the layers of cake, before she grinned sheepishly at him. "I'm sorry, as you can imagine with the music blasting, I didn't hear anything, except George Strait."

Ian grinned back at her. "Not a bad choice. Partial to him myself. How much longer will it be until the cake is done?

"At least a couple more hours. Then I'll put it into the walk-in refrigerator and head home."

"Okay, lock the door after we leave," Ian said.

"I will, thanks."

They left the baker and walked back out to the front entrance. A Scottsdale police car had parked next to Jillian's vehicle.

"Thank goodness," he whispered.

***

Jillian waited until they reached the cruiser before she introduced themselves to the officer. Ian stood in silence and waited while the policeman took her report. Her car was eventually loaded onto a flatbed tow truck and sent off to the dealership.

"Well if you can drop me off at home, I'll call first thing tomorrow for a rental car."

Ian shook his head. "Jillian, I checked in with Shawn and he believes that, given what happened, it isn't safe for me to drop you off at your house right now. Rossi appears to know way too much about your personal life, and if I left you there and anything happened, you would be a sitting duck. He suggested we put you up elsewhere."

"A hotel? Do you think that's a good idea? What if Wesley shows up tonight at my house?"

He gave her a thoughtful and sympathetic look. "I don't think that is likely to happen."

She closed her eyes. He was right. Her brother was on the run and having him just show up at home, like nothing happened, was a million-to-one long shot. She rubbed her forehead. "You're right. I still have to get my stuff and…Simon."

"Simon?"

"My cat. If I'm going away, I can't just leave him there. Cats are pretty self-sufficient, but leaving him there would be cruel."

He ran his hand through his hair. "Do you think--"

Jillian didn't let him finish. "No. If it isn't safe for me to stay there, then the cat comes with me."

"Okay."

"Although I don't know any hotels that let you bring animals with you when you check in," she added. "Any suggestions?"

"Shawn thinks the best thing to do is to have you stay at my apartment."

She opened her mouth to object, but Ian continued before she could utter a word.

"It's a one bedroom. You get the bedroom, I'll camp out on the sofa. Simon can have his pick as to who he prefers to bunk with."

From the expression on his face, Jillian could see that Ian didn't appear to be any more comfortable with the idea than she was. They'd broken up several years ago and they'd never resolved what was behind that. Now, even though Ian had been nothing but professional, living under the same roof for a couple of days would be awkward at the very least.

"I really don't want to invade your space. Besides, if I remember, you're not exactly a cat person. How long do you think we'd have to stay there?"

"I don't know," Ian replied. "Hopefully not too long. We're working hard to find Wesley."

Could this all be over quickly? Jillian had heard stories of missing people not being found for years. Were Ian and the team at the agency confident they could solve the mystery of why her brother left and where he was?

"I'll need to bring clothing for several days, a litter box, cat food, and…" She paused as she mentally rolled down a list of items. "And definitely some aspirin."

Ian crooked a grin. "Aspirin I've got. Do you cook?"

Jillian snorted a tired laugh. She got it. Ian's place was your basic bachelor pad and, if she were wise, she'd need to bring some food from her place because she guessed there wasn't much at his place. "Well, let's get this show on the road."

Chapter Eight

"Here we are. Home sweet home."

Ian unlocked his door, swung it open, and stepped back
for her to enter. Jillian cradled the carrier in her arms, walked
in a couple of steps, and stopped. She scanned the room which
included a living room, what appeared to be a galley kitchen
and small breakfast nook. What stood out was the white walls,
the carpet, also white, a few pieces of furniture and the complete
absence of anything personal. Just one generic oil painting on
the wall, no collection of personal photos, or anything else which
gave a clue as to the person who lived here. Ian Randall may have
moved into an apartment, but he clearly hadn't settled in.

"Kitchen is over here," he announced as he walked past her and
carried the grocery bags into the kitchen. She watched him disappear
into the back of the space. From the sounds of things, he'd opened the
fridge and had started placing the food she'd brought inside.

Jillian swallowed and clutched the crate holding her cat a little tighter. Maybe insisting that she bring the fruit and vegetables from the fridge was a little presumptuous, but since Ian was clear that she may not be going back home soon, leaving everything to go bad just seemed wasteful. Besides, he didn't exactly protest as she made him cart the bags of food to the car.

The fridge closed, and Ian emerged from the kitchen. "I'm going to the car to bring in another load of stuff." He glanced at her and then at the crate holding Simon. "The bedroom and the bathroom are back there."

"Okay."

Before she could say anything else, he had headed out the door and disappeared. *Yep, he's about as comfortable about this whole arrangement as you are.* Jillian walked to the back of the hall and found the bedroom. She turned on the light and surveyed the room. If she'd thought that the living and dining room had a "just moved in" vibe, then the bedroom clinched that impression. Queen-sized bed, basic linens, chest of drawers and one night stand with a lamp on it. She set the crate down beside the nightstand and then sank down to peer inside. Crystal blue eyes greeted her from the darkness of the carrier. "How are you doing, my little man?" she asked.

Simon didn't reply. Imagine that. Her oh-so-vocal Siamese cat had hunkered down in the back of the crate. She longed to open the door and let him out, but until Ian had brought in all her stuff and the front door wasn't open, she wasn't willing to risk it. A missing brother was all she could handle right now.

The front door shut and she heard footsteps coming to the master bedroom. He stopped at the door and held the emptied litter pan, with cans of cat food, a bag of litter, and the small empty food and water bowls piled in the tray. "Where should we put this?" he asked.

"We can put the litter box in the back of the bathroom and put the food in the kitchen. Will that be okay?"

Ian looked over at the crate in the corner of the room and then back to her. "Sure, I guess. I don't know much about cats. If you think that would be best for Simon, then I'm okay with it."

Jillian smiled. "Thanks."

She had to handle it to him; he was being very accommodating about the cat. She followed him out to the kitchen as he set the pet food on the counter. He looked up as she stood at the entrance of the kitchen and stopped. "Here, you go ahead and set this up for your cat. I have one more trip to the car."

"I can help you," Jillian volunteered.

"No. Stay here and get the cat's stuff set up. I think that it would be best if you weren't too visible." He paused. "Just in case someone is watching."

Fear fingered its way down her back as the meaning of the last comment registered. "All right," she replied as she stepped aside and allowed Ian to pass her.

He didn't comment, but went straight to the door and left for another trip to the car. "This is going to be so awkward," she muttered.

By the time he'd returned, she had set up the food for the cat and had almost finished setting up the litter box in the bathroom. Ian didn't comment as he walked back to the bedroom and left her luggage there.

When Jillian finished, she found Ian still in the bedroom. The top chest of drawers was open, and he was pulling out a gun and holster. She froze and watched him pull it out and load up the magazine into it. He handled the weapon with a comfort and ease that was a bit scary and exciting at the same time. She had to admit that she had no experience with guns, but clearly Ian was on the other end of the spectrum. Feeling the need to break the silence, she cleared her throat. "What type of gun is that?"

"Glock."

She didn't know what to say next, and Ian wasn't making any effort to talk. For several seconds she watched him and racked her mind for something to say. Finally she succumbed to stating the obvious. "Are you going to be carrying a gun from this point forward?"

He looked up and nodded. "The damage to your car was a message. Rossi won't be willing to wait forever for us to find your brother or get his money. Even though you reported what he had said to the police, this guy may be hard to find. So yes, I thing carrying a gun is a prudent thing to do."

"Do you think Wesley has left town?"

"Don't know. Hopefully something will break soon."

Jillian's stomach growled. "I'm going to fix something to eat. Do you want something?"

Ian holstered his weapon and closed the dresser drawer. "Yeah that would be nice. What were you thinking about?"

"I don't know. Something light. Soup, maybe a sandwich." She paused as he walked toward her and stopped. "Would that be okay?"

He cracked a small smile. "That would be great. I'm afraid I'm not much of a cook, but the good news is I'm not terribly picky. Whatever you want to fix will be fine."

Jillian studied his face. He appeared tired and a five o'clock shadow graced his jaw. The impulse to walk over and trace her finger along his jawline niggled at her, and she tamped it down.

"Let me let Simon out so he can explore and get his bearings." She stepped around him, headed over to the carrier and opened the wire door.

"Is there anything we need to do for him?" Ian asked.

"No, just give him a bit of space and let him explore. I just want him to locate the food, water, and litter box soon."

Even with the carrier open, the cat didn't emerge.

"He's not coming out." Ian said.

"He will," Jillian said as she rose to her feet. "Let's go fix dinner."

***

Ian sucked in a slow breath and let it out in an effort to dial down his senses that were so amped right now that they crackled like an electrical switch having been flipped on. He should have insisted that they put up Jillian and her cat at a hotel. There had to be hundreds in the Valley. Surely they could have evaded Rossi's watchful eye. Now with Jillian here in his eight hundred and forty square foot one-bedroom, he was keenly aware of everything about her.

He rubbed his forehead and closed his eyes. What had Shawn been thinking when he suggested this? Look at what happened when he had shared the same roof with Morgan as they evaded her stalker. *Did he recommend this option on purpose?*

"Oh man," he whispered.

Tomorrow, when he could get a chance, he'd have a long talk

with his older brother. He and Jillian were history and no amount of being together would change that. The sooner his brother understood that, the better.

Sudden movement out of the corner of his eye made him stiffen in surprise before he figured out what it was. Simon had left the carrier and had started a slow, cautious exploration of the bedroom.

The cat traveled to the corner of his bed and hunkered down to stare at him. Ian couldn't read 'cat', but the animal appeared to be assessing him. "Hey, buddy. Welcome to your new digs."

Tail twitching back and forth, the cat continued to study him, slowly reinforcing Ian's impression that some level of feline evaluation was taking place. Maybe petting the cat might break the ice between the two of them. Ian took a step forward and stopped. Simon held his ground. Ian took a second step, and as if he hit some invisible trip-wire, the cat spun, scrambled and disappeared.

"Great," Ian muttered. He took a quick scan around the room and concluded that the cat had either retreated back into the carrier or had made a beeline under the bed. Either way, he had no desire to rev up the cat any more than he already was.

"Well, Simon, when you're ready to come out from where ever you are. Your mom is in the kitchen. She's fixing a meal for us, and your dinner is already waiting for you."

Ian turned and started down the hallway. He sensed he was being watched and threw a glance over his shoulder. The cat sat on the carpeting in the doorway. Ian smirked and walked away.

He rounded the corner and found Jillian in full-blown Martha Stewart mode. She'd managed to find the pans, open a can of soup, and was putting the finishing touches on what looked to be ham and Swiss cheese sandwiches.

She looked up as he stood at the entry of the galley kitchen. "Dinner will be ready shortly."

Jillian moved with the confidence and efficiency of a professional chef. After a couple tries, she located the dinner plates and soup bowls, and began to plate the sandwiches and ladle the soup.

Ian crooked a grin. This might not be all bad after all. Granted, he was so hyperaware of Jillian's presence that he could have located her in total darkness, but at least he wasn't going to starve.

Jillian caught his smile. "What?"

"Nothing," Ian replied.

She snorted a laugh. "Oh come on. I know that tone of voice. You're thinking about something." She looked down at the food she'd just finished up preparing, and a soft smile bloomed. She pointed to the food. "Is this okay?"

Ian threaded his hand through his hair and nodded. "This is fine. As I said before, I'm not picky. What you've fixed so far is far beyond what I throw together for dinner."

"I kind of thought that."

Ian's smile faded. "Oh?

"Because your fridge and pantry have little to no food in them. I'm betting you're a take-out kind of guy."

Ian grinned. "Sounds like you discovered my drawer of menus."

Jillian handed him the plates with the sandwiches and turned to pick up the soup bowls. "Yeah. I wasn't snooping. Really, I was just trying to find the silverware, and I found your stash."

Ian stepped over and placed the plates on the glass-top dinette table. Jillian walked up beside him and set the bowls down. "Go ahead, take a seat," she said over her shoulder as she returned to the kitchen to retrieve the soup spoons and napkins.

Ian pulled out a chair. He sank into it and waited until she returned and took a seat before picking up a spoon and stirring his soup.

He glanced at her, and she smiled before picking up her spoon. They ate for a couple of minutes in silence. Simon appeared in the living room.

"Well look who's decided to join us for dinner," Ian remarked.

Jillian twisted around in her seat and caught the cat slowly exploring around the sofa and coffee table. "Ignore him. If we make a fuss, he may retreat back to the bedroom."

"Too late."

She looked up from her plate. "What happened?"

"Well, he emerged from his carrier and when I went over to pet him, I must have scared him because he made a dash for cover. I think he went under the bed."

Jillian smiled. "He's usually not easily spooked, but with all the changes, I think he's also a little rattled."

We're all a little rattled. Ian didn't comment and took a bite of his sandwich, and then asked, "In high school, your family had dogs. When did you get a cat?"

She paused as she finished off what she was chewing, and then took a moment before responding. "I had just broken up with my boyfriend and was alone in my condo. With the crazy hours I keep, getting a cat was the logical pet choice."

"Did you get him from a cat breeder?"

"Nope. He's an adoption from one of the no-kill shelters in town. When I started looking, I searched their list of cats up for adoption and there he was. Until Wes moved in, it was just the two of us. Wes isn't exactly a 'cat person' so he pretty much ignored Simon while he was there."

"Did Wes go out much?"

Jillian set the spoon down. "Occasionally. Why do you ask?"

"Just wondering if there was a favorite watering hole that he liked to frequent."

She studied him. "You're thinking about something. What is it?"

Ian leaned over the table toward Jillian. "Well, it was something that Ashley said earlier this afternoon. She'd mentioned that Wes and Roger had a 'boy's night out' from time to time. I think she knows more than she is willing to reveal, at least until she talks to Roger about what they want to tell us. I was wondering if Wesley ever mentioned where they went when he went out with the guys."

Jillian pressed her lips together as she considered his question. "Honestly, Wes never discussed much of what he did when he went out. I know that this sounds like I wasn't paying attention, but I'm not his mother. A fact that he not-so-kindly reminded me when I asked too many questions from time to time."

"If Rossi is correct, and Wesley forged your information on a loan, your brother committed identity theft and he has now made his business your business."

Jillian slumped back in her chair and paused. "You're right. I gave him trust and space to run his life, and it appears that he has made a mess of it. Heck, I made a mess of it. I should be have been more attentive to what was going on. I assumed that he'd kicked his drug addiction, and he was settling in to a normal life. I was wrong."

Her eyes welled with tears. Ian's chest tightened. He'd made her cry, again. He appeared to have an annoying talent for it, considering that every time he asked questions about her brother, he never realized when he crossed over some emotional trip wire.

"Oh God, I'm sorry," he said wearily.

Jillian nodded. "I know. It's so frustrating." She stood and her chair tumbled back behind her. "You all must think I'm an idiot. How could I have missed the signs?"

"Jilli…"

"You haven't called me that in…forever."

Ian placed his napkin on the table and stood. "I'm sorry. It seems all I'm doing is rubbing salt in the wounds."

She nodded and grabbed her napkin to wipe her eyes. "Not your fault. It's your job to dig for information that may have been overlooked."

Jillian stepped toward him and touched his forearm, and then as if she realized that she shouldn't, she pulled back.

"Don't," Ian said in a voice that was barely above a whisper. "Don't let go."

He captured her arm and drew her to him. As he wrapped his arms around her, he felt her rigid posture melt. A faint fragrance from a perfume applied long ago registered, light and floral.

Ian softened his hold, and she nestled against his chest. She fit perfectly in his embrace as she wrapped her arms around him and her head tucked under his chin. "Oh Jilli, it's been a long time."

She didn't respond and continued to hold on to him. Memories flooded his mind of them together years ago. What had happened? It had been so perfect and yet after they graduated high school, they had drifted and went their separate ways. No it had been more than that. Far more than that. There had been fights. He wanted to get married, and she wasn't ready. Jillian wanted to go to college, to work, to travel. In the end, she went out of state to pursue her degree. But as time moved on, they talked less and less. Then he was told by her sister that she was dating someone she'd met at college. He'd figured that she'd left him behind and he made the choice to join the military. Now, years later, she'd done all that she'd planned to do. She had her dream and he was left with nightmares of what he'd seen and done.

Slowly she pulled back and looked up. Her gaze warm. "Yes, it has."

Ian lowered his head and kissed her. Her lips were soft and welcoming. His fingers traveled up and across her jaw till they threaded into her hair, soft and silky. Now that he had his hands on her, she wasn't going anywhere. A soft whimper escaped from her as his tongue gently pressed. In the distance, he heard a ring.

Phone ringing. His, or hers? Irritation crackled through Ian as he pulled back and checked his phone that was attached in a carrier to his belt. "Not mine."

He chuffed a breath of air in frustration as Jillian pulled back and moved slowly to her purse, which sat on the table by the door.

Ian studied her as she answered her phone. She looked totally hot, mussy, and thoroughly kissed. Had the phone not rang, he would have done his best to keep on kissing her.

CHAPTER NINE

"Roger, thank you for calling."

"Speaker phone," Ian mouthed to her, and Jillian nodded and pressed the button.

"Roger, I've put you on the speaker phone so Ian Randall, from Sonoran Security, can also hear our conversation."

"Ashley told me you stopped by the house this afternoon and that Wes is missing. What happened?" Roger asked.

"Roger, Ian Randall here. Wes's disappearance caught Jillian and her family totally off guard. We're looking for more information about Wesley so we can locate him. Could you help us? Do you know of any places he liked to frequent?"

A pause filled the air for a few moments, and Jillian thought that perhaps Roger was about to clam up on them. Then he replied, "Ian, when he came over we usually hung out around the house and watched sports, and had barbecue. Occasionally, some of the other guys I know from work would have a guys' night out. Basically pretty harmless, tame stuff, if you know what I mean."

"How often was the guys' night out?" Ian asked.

"Oh, I don't know. Maybe once every two or three months. Not that often."

Jillian interjected. "Where did you guys go?"

"It varied. Sometimes we'd go to a baseball or basketball game. Couple of times we just went to a casino on the reservation for drinks and a little gambling. No crazy stuff Most of us have mortgages."

Jillian shook her head. Despite Roger's cooperation, the information wasn't turning out to be as insightful as she'd hoped.

"Do you know anyone named Joe Rossi?" Ian asked.

"Joe Rossi?" Roger repeated. "No, the name isn't familiar. Why do you ask?"

"Jillian has received a couple of phone calls from him. He's looking for Wes too."

"Hmm. Wes never mentioned anyone by that name. At least not as I can recall," Roger said.

"Could you provide us the names and phone numbers of the guys that participated on the guys' night out events?" Jillian asked.

Ian smiled at her, giving her a thumbs up.

"Sure," Roger replied. "Let me sit down and write up a list of the guys and I can email it over to you. Will that be okay?"

"I've got a sheet of paper here on this end. It's no problem, I can take the info now," Jillian said. "Roger, I think Wes is in some kind of trouble, and if we don't find him soon, we're very concerned that something bad may happen."

There was a pause on the other end of the phone. "Uh, okay,"

Roger replied. "This may not be an exactly complete list since I'm kind of doing this on the fly."

"Thanks. I'm sure that this will be a great help," Jillian replied.

The next few minutes were spent with Roger recounting what events they had done during the last five months, and the list of people who attended. Jillian was disappointed to some degree, because the group of attendees was small, usually three or four men with the exception of either Roger or her brother. There didn't seem to be a core group who went to each and every event.

"Roger, was Wesley using drugs?"

Jillian's head snapped up from the notes she was writing as she fired Ian a surprised look. She opened her mouth to speak and Ian raised a finger to his lips urging silence.

"Oh, God no. I don't think so. I suppose it is possible. I mean the casinos have gambling, alcohol, and I suppose other stuff could be available. However, Wesley never appeared to be 'on anything.'"

"Thanks for your information and time," Ian replied. "I don't have any more questions, but we'd like to be able to get back in touch with you if we think of anything else."

He looked over to her. "Jillian, do you have anything else to ask?"

She stared at him for a few seconds before answering. "No. I'm good. Thank you, Roger."

"No problem. If I can be of further help, please let me know," Roger responded.

Within seconds Jillian discontinued the phone call and set the smart phone down. "Okay, would you mind telling me what that was about?"

"The question about Wesley using drugs?"

"Exactly."

"I was interested in seeing if Roger would confirm your opinion that Wesley had not suffered a relapse and I wanted to see how he would respond to that question. Roger and your brother go way back. He knew Wesley before things got out of hand. He would have a good feel on this issue."

Jillian exhaled and leaned back in the chair. "Well he said no on that count."

"Yep, he did. But he said something that was interesting. He indicated that he could have scored drugs while in the casino. Casinos, even the ones in Arizona, are wired to the teeth with surveillance cameras. They watch the employees, the gambling areas, hallways, and all entrances and exits. If they'd observed someone dealing, they would stop it and quick."

She looked at Ian who returned her gaze and nodded. "It makes sense. So what are you thinking?"

"I'm not sure. Working on it."

"So our next step is?"

Ian glanced at his wrist watch. "Nothing tonight. It's getting late and you've got a busy day tomorrow. Here, let me get the dishes."

He stood and carted his dishes to the kitchen. Jillian followed him into the kitchen and prepared to rinse and load the dishes into the dishwasher.

Ian took the plates from her hands. "I've got this. I'm going to take a shower when I'm done. Do you want to use the bathroom first?"

"No. But while you're in the bathroom, I'll change into something else and grab some sheets for the sofa."

"Thanks." Jillian strolled out of the kitchen and out of view. Ian made a point to not watch her walk away. *That's the second person who said Wesley wasn't using drugs. If they're right, why is Wesley on the run from a man who deals drugs?*

CHAPTER TEN

Ian arranged the sheets, blanket, and pillow and turned on the television. In the distance he could hear the shower going. *Jillian here. In his shower, soon to be sleeping in his bed.* A buzz hummed through him as if he were hooked up to the power grid. Ian gave the pillow a firm punch. "Come on. Get a grip," he growled as he sank back down on the sofa and grabbed the TV remote. He scrolled through the stations, looking for something to catch his interest and settled on a news channel.

As the announcer ticked off short segments on the top incidents of the day, his mind wandered back over what had happened today. Something had been brewing for quite a while in regards to Wesley's life and he'd managed to hide it well from Jillian.

He heard the water stop in the bathroom, and he glanced over and found Simon on the window ledge surveying the world outside of the apartment. Ian wondered if he should catch the cat and make sure that he was corralled in the bedroom with Jillian or would it would be better to let him have the run of the apartment? When Jillian was out, he'd ask.

His eyes traveled back to the television screen. Footage of recent activities in the Middle East flashed across the screen and the host began to update them about a suicide bomber who happened to detonate a vest of explosives while situated within a marketplace. The numbers of the injured and killed were matter-of-factly reported. He pressed his lips together. *It's never going to stop.*

He heard the bathroom door open and then the bedroom door close. Ian decided to give her a few minutes before knocking on the door and asking about the cat. Clicking the remote, he started pulled up the schedule and searched for something else to watch.

"I think that we need to set a schedule for tomorrow."

Ian looked up and found Jillian standing at the entrance of the living room. She was wearing silky blue pajamas with a robe over the top that was firmly belted closed. It didn't matter. Wisps of damp hair clung to her neck and her face had a rosy flush. Ian swallowed. *Focus.*

"Good idea." He sat up on the sofa and muted the TV. "Since you have the wedding tomorrow, what time do you need to be there and when do you anticipate that things will be over?"

"The wedding isn't until four. I would prefer to get there around eight in the morning. The crew will be coming in at ten to start prepping for the party and dinner. It will be late into the evening before we'll be cleaning things up and closing down."

Ian nodded. "How long do the wedding receptions usually run?"

"It can depend upon the party. Some people stay, drink, dance, and party. Other times, once the bride and groom leave, things can wind down pretty quickly."

"Based upon your experience, what will this group be like?"

"Probably somewhere in the middle. It I had to bet, I'm thinking things will wind down between nine to nine-thirty."

"Okay. I'll take you to work. I may hang around until your crew starts showing up. You should be safe at the Villa with a lot of people around you. I need to go into the office and check in with the team. Perhaps we'll have a breakthrough. Will that work?"

Jillian nodded. "That would be fine."

Ian pointed over to her cat. "What about him? Do you want him in the bedroom with you or should we let him have the run of the apartment?"

She looked over at her Siamese and considered the question. "He appears to have settled down. The litter box is in the bathroom and food and water are in the kitchen. If I confine him in the bedroom, we'll need to move all that into the bedroom. Would you mind if we let him have run of the apartment?"

"No," Ian replied.

"Thanks." Jillian reached up and swept her hair back away from her face. "If there is nothing else we need to discuss, I'll see you in the morning. Good night."

"Night," Ian said.

With his reply, she turned and walked back to the bedroom. A chill settled over him. As if when she left she sucked the warmth from him. The sound of the bedroom door carried down the hall. He picked up the remote, turned the television and lights off, and settled in the sofa. He stared as the screen until his eyelids became heavy.

The dust clouded the air. Even within the enclosed armored vehicle, it seeped in through every crack. Ian rolled his head in a circular motion, stretching his neck muscles as he looked at what little could be seen from the few windows in the armored vehicle. Raul sat across from him and a light glaze of sweat gave his face a glossy sheen. To his right, Will shifted and adjusted his flack jacket before checking his weapon for what may have been the hundredth time. Thomas was situated in the crow's nest. He watched the activity in the town and kept an eye out for any suspicious behavior.

The patrol had been quiet, too quiet for Ian's taste. The streets, even though they patrolled during the day, were near empty. In his mind, the stillness lent an air of impending doom.

Ian had heard that the hardest part of a tour was the final weeks and days before you went back home. Home, oh dear God, he was ready to go home. He'd been ready for months. To get away from the suspicious looks from the civilians, the uncertainty of who was a friend or foe, and the violence and death. The fact that he was so close to getting out in one piece made him scared. The deepest fear that despite everything, the law of averages would swing against him and he'd end up injured or dead.

Thomas coughed. He reached for a bottled water and took a swig. He set the bottle down into the holder and commented, "We're almost there."

"How does it look?" Raul asked.

"Okay," Thomas replied.

Ian caught the discomfort in Thomas' voice.

A thunderous explosion slammed against the tank. Even in the vehicle, the force of the blast rocked the crew. No one spoke for a second. They didn't have to. An IUD had gone off and their vehicle stopped.

"Talk to me, Tom," Ian said.

"Looks like it hit a couple of vehicles up. I can't see how bad it is." *Ian's chest tightened as he scanned the faces of the men in the carrier. He could see the anger bubbling in each of them. Will hissed a curse under his breath about the Taliban and Raul nodded in agreement.*

"Get ready," Thomas ordered.

Each of them knew what that meant. They picked up their weapons and prepped to leave the vehicle. Within seconds, Thomas began to feed them detailed information of what they would see. He ID'd a middle-aged man in a dark sweater who had stood by the side of the road and didn't flinch or seem alarmed when the bomb detonated.

"He knows or has seen something. Let's pick him up," Thomas said.

The door at the back of the vehicle opened and they slid out. Ian knew the drill. He'd done it many times before. You didn't race out of the vehicle in hot pursuit. You emerged slowly, providing cover and watching every quarter. You looked for people who didn't belong. Civilians like the 'sweater man' who without any apparent reason just seemed to be standing in the right place, or conversely, you sought out those who scurried away before all hell broke loose.

The trio walked in front of the armor-reinforced Hummer and into the intersection, setting up an impromptu check-point for vehicles or pedestrians. An ancient beaten up white Buick cruised to a stop, and Raul, after a quick visual inspection, allowed it to proceed down the pothole-ridden dirt road. Ian surveyed the streets. The buildings, for the most part, were one-story and blended into the desert sand. Not well maintained. In fact, with the rubble and discarded junk that littered the street, the place looked crap-freakin-tacular. Many of the residences were surrounded with high brick fences that prohibited seeing what was behind them.

Sweater man. Will pointed to the man slowly fading back into a side street. The Iraqi knew better than to run. That would have drawn immediate attention and pursuit. But his casual slow walk wasn't fast enough to make a complete disappearance. Ian met Will's gaze and nodded. They were off. No need to run after him, just walk faster and they'd catch up with him soon enough.

Within a minute, they had caught up with the man. He looked at Will and then at Ian. Distrust and thinly veiled fear glittered in his eyes. At times like this, Ian wished he could speak the local language. But no such luck. Will made a radio request for an interpreter. They walked the Iraqi man back to the armored vehicle.

Soon two soldiers appeared and, with the four men surrounding the civilian, the interrogation began. Ian's attention alternated between watching and listening to the conversation and surveying the street. "Hurry up," the voice in his head warned. They'd been out and exposed on the streets far too long for his taste and, if anything were to erupt, it would get ugly way too fast.

"Okay," the soldier who came with the interpreter said. "He says he lives over there in that building and that he was going to cross the intersection but when we came through with the vehicles he decided to stop and wait."

"So what do we do now?" Will asked.

"We're going to escort him back to his house and maybe check things out a bit."

"You need us to help?" Ian asked.

"Nope, we'll take it from here."

"How bad was it up there?" Will asked.

"We were lucky. It was a small IUD. Some damage to the vehicle, and minor injuries."

Ian felt the knot in his stomach loosen a notch. He checked on Raul, who was in the process of letting a small green import car pass through the intersection. Then, out of the corner of his eye, he saw the white Buick come back from the other direction through the intersection.

"What the...." He never got a chance to finish the words. The vehicle picked up speed and barreled down on the officer in the middle of the street. "Raul, look out!"

Raul turned and scurried out of the path, but the driver adjusted and barreled down on the soldier. Ian raised his rifle, and when he had a clear line of sight, fired.

"Ian." He felt a hand on his chest. "Ian, wake up."

He gasped and lurched up, grasping the arm. The shadow of a person struggled against his grasp, and he snapped his hand around the person's other arm.

"Let me go!"

A woman's voice, filled with anger and panic, registered inside his head. "Ian, let me go!"

Jillian. He let go. She fell back and landed on the carpet between the coffee table and the end of the sofa. He heard a crash as if something had been knocked over. But he sat up, stared into the darkness, and sucked in rapid breaths of air.

The lamp on the end table snapped on. Jillian stood staring at him, rubbing her wrists. *Jillian, oh God what did I do?*

"I'm sorry," he gasped. "I'm so sorry. Are you okay?"

"Yeah," she replied.

He studied her. She'd not bothered to put on her robe, and her chestnut-colored hair hung in an unruly mess around her shoulders. The pajama top was loosely askew, showing her collar bone. She sank into the chair and massaged her wrists.

"Are you okay?" she asked.

No. He studied her for a couple seconds. "Yes. I must have had a nightmare."

Jillian dropped her hands and regarded him. Concern graced her eyes. "It must have been a doozy. You were shouting out. You scared the heck out of me. I thought for a second or two maybe Rossi or some of his guys had shown up."

Ian dropped his head into his hands. "No, it was only a nightmare."

He raised his face and looked at her wrists. They were red and he wondered if bruises would develop. Guilt settled over him like a lead blanket. He wasn't a perfect man, not by any stretch of the imagination, but violence against a woman wasn't in his character.

"Wanna talk about it?"

Ian shook his head. No, he didn't. But maybe Shawn was right, and he should check out seeing a therapist. Clearly this problem wasn't going away; in fact, it might be getting worse.

He surveyed the living room. "Where's Simon?"

"Not sure, probably hiding under a piece of furniture somewhere."

As if he'd heard his name and wanted to join the conversation, the cat appeared at the entrance to the hall to the bedroom.

"Poor boy, probably scared the daylights out of him."

Jillian smiled. "He'll be okay. The question is, will you? Does this happen often?"

Ian took a deep breath and exhaled. "From time to time. Sometimes it's a nightmare and other times it can happen when I'm awake. It's weird. The strangest things can trigger my visions. A couple days back, the thunderstorm did it."

He stared at the cat, avoiding Jillian's gaze. She leaned forward and gently laid her hand on his forearm. He glanced down at her hand.

"Ian, you need to get some help. I'm no expert, but it sounds like you have PTSD."

"Yeah, I've heard that one before."

"No, I'm serious. If this is happening a lot you should seek some therapy or counseling."

Ian pulled away from her. "I'll be fine." He looked away, refusing to look into her eyes, scared he'd see pity.

Several seconds of silence passed, then Jillian stood up and walked back to the bedroom. Ian rolled back and sank into the sofa, face vertical, and stared at the white ceiling. "Great, I'm crazy. Welcome home, soldier, and thank you for your service."

CHAPTER ELEVEN

Ian opened his eyes and smelled coffee. *Thank you Jillian.* She must have gone into the kitchen and started brewing a pot, and he was going to need the caffeine today.

Taking a deep breath, he exhaled and slowly rose from the sofa. He had no clue when he had finally dozed back off. After Jillian had returned to the bedroom, he had turned on the television and spent who knows how long watching old sitcoms until finally he drifted off.

He stood and stretched and came to the conclusion that the sofa, while not quite as good as a regular bed, made an acceptable alternative place to sleep. He walked over to the kitchen. Two clean empty mugs sat on the counter next to the coffee maker. Simon had finished what must have been some canned cat food and sauntered up and rubbed himself across the sweatpants that covered Ian's legs. "Well, you've decided that I'm not so bad, right?" Ian asked.

The cat rubbed the side of his face on the fleece. Ian slowly bent over and stroked the cat's back. The Siamese vibrated with a purr and arched his back.

"Good morning."

Ian stood up and turned to find Jillian standing there behind him. She'd clearly been up for a while as she had dressed and fixed her hair and make-up. Gone were the suits and today Jillian wore a royal blue dress that was shorter than what he'd seen her in before. It managed to showcase her legs.

She smiled. "Looks like Simon likes you."

Ian grinned. "Yeah. Thanks for making the coffee. I'll pour. How do you like yours?"

"Sugar and cream."

"Not sure I have cream." Ian walked over to the fridge, hoping that maybe skim milk would do if the carton expiration date hadn't come and gone.

"I brought over a small carton from my place," Jillian said.

He opened the door and scanned the contents. Weird, there was food in there. A fair amount, so much that it took him some time to locate the cream that Jillian said she'd brought. After a few seconds, he pulled it out and walked over to the counter.

Jillian had kept her distance and had not walked into the kitchen. He pretended not to notice. Her behavior was understandable. If he'd been in her shoes and went through what happened last night, he'd put some space between them too.

After pouring a cup, he handed it to her along with a spoon and pushed the sugar bowl and carton of cream closer. "I don't know how much you like to add."

"Thanks." Jillian took the cup, set it down, and added what she wanted.

He poured a cup for himself and looked over at her. "I'm sorry about last night. I'm going into the office later this morning, and if you would feel more comfortable with someone else with you, I'll request a re-assignment."

Jillian took a sip and then answered. "No. I want you to stay." She crooked a small smile. "Besides if things get out of hand, I know that you'll know how to deal with it." Her smile faded. "Provided you feel comfortable."

Ian nodded. "I'll be fine. You may have a point about getting some help. Shawn suggested that too." He paused and concentrated on adding sugar to his coffee. "In transitioning to civilian life. Not that I'm losing it," He added quietly.

Jillian locked eyes with him. "You're not losing it. I think it haunts you. I've read that this is far more common for returning soldiers than people realize and I've read somewhere they've developed a number of therapies to help."

He watched her as she set the mug down. She quietly traced her finger up and down the side. "It's not any of my business so I won't ask, but I know you and you're a decent guy who has been through a lot. You need to come to terms with what happened over there."

Ian set the mug down and nodded slowly. "Give me thirty minutes, and I'll be ready to take you to work."

Jillian stepped back from the kitchen entrance so he could exit. "Take your time."

***

While he shaved and got dressed, Jillian sat at the dining room table and sipped her coffee. When Ian offered this morning to get re-assigned, she had to give him credit for recognizing his episode last night had scared the daylights out of her. But she didn't want him to leave.

She followed the news and read the magazines and cable articles. From what was reported, the troops were under constant siege. Never truly safe, even when back at their bases.

Jillian leaned back into the chair and glanced out the window. Something would break soon in regards to Wesley's disappearance. She didn't know exactly what, but she could feel it in her bones.

Ian entered the living room. He wore gray dress slacks and a shirt and tie. Jillian had to admit, the man cleaned up well. But what caught her attention was a glimpse of what looked like suspenders. But on second glance, she realized they weren't suspenders. *He's got a shoulder holster and he's carrying the Glock.* She swallowed as she recalled what she said earlier this morning. *Besides, if things get out of hand, I know that you'll know how to deal with it.*

"Do you think that we'll need that?" she asked quietly.

Ian shrugged into his jacket. "I'm hoping not. Right now, I'm concerned as to what Rossi may do next if we don't find your brother."

Jillian didn't respond to his comment. Instead, she stood up, took her mug to the kitchen, and set it in the sink while offering a silent prayer that they would find Wes soon, and in one piece.

Within minutes, they had locked up the apartment and went to Ian's car.

They rode in silence on the way into work. Ian didn't want to talk and cranked up the radio to make conversation impossible.

She glanced down at her wristwatch. Seven-thirty. By the time they arrived, Larry, the head chef, should be there. There were over one hundred and fifty guests to serve and they would start the prep several hours ahead of the event.

As they pulled into the parking lot of La Villa de Gardenia, she scanned the parking lot. Nothing looked amiss. In fact, she could see Larry's car on the side of the building.

Ian turned down the radio. "I'll escort you in. Once in, I'd like it if we could do a quick tour of the facility and see that everything is in place and that no one who shouldn't be there is hanging around. If all is good, I'll head off to the office. Don't leave the facility and if anything crops up, call me. Okay?"

"Fine," Jillian replied.

As they entered the front entrance, she could see that the maintenance crew were adding white lights to the olive trees in the courtyard.

"Let me drop off my purse and stuff in my office and then we'll make the rounds."

Ian nodded and walked with her to her office in silence. Something about him had changed from yesterday. It was if he was on high alert. Was he still rattled from last night? She snuck a peek and caught him silently surveying the covered hallways. His eyes were constantly searching every corner or space hidden behind a bush or shrub. Her stomach tightened as she realized he expected something to have happened, or worse, someone to be here. She followed his gaze to the hallway in shadows from the second floor. Maybe last night with her car vandalized, she should have insisted that she make the tour of the facility for any other problems. She would have picked up any problems more quickly than Ian.

As they approached the entrance to the building, she rummaged in her purse and fished out her keys. Once she entered the main building, she deactivated the alarm and began to walk the short distance to her office.

Ian let her unlock the door. Then he reached up and touched her. "Let me go first."

Jillian stepped back as he opened the door slowly and entered the room. Seconds passed as she strained to hear any noises. For a man as large as Ian, he was silent as he moved around the office. *Silence. That's good.* A few seconds later, the desk lamp at her desk switched on and she peered in.

"All clear. Come on in."

She quickly moved to her desk, placed her purse in the lower left drawer, and her tote bag on the floor behind the desk.

"I need to check in with the kitchen."

"Let's go."

As they approached, she could hear the radio playing rock music. She opened the door and canvassed the room. Two chefs stood near the sink prepping vegetables. "Where's Larry?"

The older of the two cooks looked up and pointed over to the walk-in refrigerator. She glanced up to Ian. "I've got this. You can leave for the office."

"I'll call and check in later."

Jillian stepped through the doorway and, as she went to close the door, she paused and watch Ian walk across the courtyard. As the distance between them widened, a sense of longing increased. She wished she could call him back, have him near. But to do so would be silly. She exhaled and closed the kitchen door.

Jillian walked across the kitchen. The large metal door to the walk-in refrigerator was open and she peered in. Larry stood over in the corner where the steaks were stored, with a clipboard in his hand.

"Hi, how's it going?"

The man looked up. "Okay, I guess. I'm just getting ready to pull the meat out for seasoning, and it looks like we're missing some steaks."

"I thought you made a count when the food arrived yesterday. Did we get shorted?"

"I did make a count and we got what we ordered," the chef replied as he shook his head. "But look." He pointed to the top box nearest to the corner. "That one has been opened, and when I checked, we're missing a couple of steaks."

"That's strange. It's not happened before," Jillian said.

"I know. The only person here last night was Mary. I can't imagine that she took them."

"Are we going to be okay or do we need a rush order?"

"No, I think that we'll be okay. I always order several extra steaks. You never know when someone will send a steak back because it's too well done or something like that. Give me five minutes and let me do a quick recount, and I'll confirm."

Jillian looked at her watch. "Okay, let me know where we stand."

She then turned and headed to the courtyard to check in with the maintenance teams. *Who could have taken those steaks?*

Chapter Twelve

They know something. The thought pinged through Ian's mind as he scanned the room and looked at the team who had assembled in the conference room. He pulled a sesame bagel out and added some veggie cream cheese, pretending to focus on preparing it and waiting to see who, if any, of the tech team would spill the beans.

"Good morning," Shawn said as he walked into the conference room. Matt followed silently behind him. Both men sat down and waited a few seconds while Ian took his seat.

"Updates?" Matt asked.

Thomas and Paul looked at each other and then grinned. "We've found Wesley's BMW."

Ian rapidly gulped down the bite of bagel. "Where?"

"Just where we thought it might be, down at one of the fleabag rent-by-the-hour hotels on Van Buren." Thomas replied.

"Okay." Ian nodded. "Was Wesley there?"

"No." Paul said. "We checked with the manager and he says that Wesley paid for a week, but he hasn't seen him."

"We don't know if the manager is covering for him or if that's the truth," Thomas added.

"If the two of you are here, who's watching the hotel?" Matt asked.

The cocky grins evaporated. Paul admitted, "Sabrina."

Matt scowled. "So you're saying that you left an attractive twenty-two year old woman down in an area populated with prostitutes, pimps, and drug dealers, all alone?"

Both of the younger men went stone silent, and for once Ian enjoyed watching someone else squirm on the hot seat.

"Things are pretty quiet during daylight hours. Both of us have been up all night taking rounds and waiting to see if Ms. Connors' brother would return." Paul responded. "Besides, Sabrina can take care of herself."

Matt shook his head and leaned back in his seat. "I don't like this. Not one bit, gentlemen."

Ian shot a quick glance at his brother, who sat watching the exchange silently. As if Shawn sensed his brother's gaze, he looked briefly at Ian, then glanced down and flipped through the papers he had laid out in front of him.

"We also placed a tracking device on the car. So if he does come back to retrieve the car and we miss him, we can find out where he is."

"All right," Shawn said. "Ian, can you update the team on what has happened with Ms. Connors?"

Ian took the next few minutes and recapped the discovery that

Wesley had been terminated from his job, the threats from Rossi, and the vandalism to Jillian's car. He'd expected that someone would have taken the opportunity to comment about the fact that she had spent the night at his apartment, but no one appeared to give it a second thought. He finished up by informing the team that there was a wedding scheduled at the Villa and Jillian and the staff were in the final stages of prepping for the event.

"So did Sabrina have any luck at the pawn shops before she was put on surveillance?" Ian asked.

"No," Paul replied. "Nothing yet, but if Wesley Connors has a substance abuse issue, then it would only be a matter of time before something would turn up, provided he started selling the stuff."

"You know, I'm not so sure that there is a drug issue. I mean there could be, but this doesn't explain where Rossi fits into this picture. He keeps insisting that Wesley owes him fifty thousand."

"Good point," Shawn replied. "We have a little more intelligence on Joseph Rossi."

Ian had heard the phrase, "could have heard a pin drop", but the room actually became so quiet after his brother's comment that he believed you actually could have heard one hit the carpet.

"Looks like Mr. Rossi is an entrepreneur with many business interests. He may still be involved with drugs, and quite possibly prostitution and illegal gambling."

"Great," Matt said dryly. "Do you think Wesley chose the hotel on purpose so that he could connect with Rossi?"

"Not sure," Ian said. "I suppose that's possible, but it would be highly risky. I mean, Rossi may decide that if Connors wasn't good for the money, he just might make an example of him to others owing him money."

"Well, if Jillian's brother has dropped off the grid, maybe Rossi figures his best chance of getting paid is to squeeze Jillian."

With that comment, his brother leveled his gaze at Ian. "Does Jillian have the money to pay Rossi off if she has to?"

"Not sure. She might. But if she does, it's probably not sitting in some checking account somewhere. It may take a few days to sell stocks or something like that."

Matt piped up. "You might want to give her a heads-up that may have to take place. I mean, we're not exactly SEAL-team six here. If this things gets to the point of 'pay or someone gets hurt', she may have to find a way to get the funds. We'll work with the police on this, but…" The sandy-haired Texan's voice trailed off into silence.

"I'll let her know," Ian said. He scanned the faces of the four people in the room. The excitement about discovering Wesley's car had melted into silence.

"I'm going back to La Villa de Gardenia to keep an eye on Jillian. She's already told the police about Rossi when her car was trashed. From the police standpoint, this is a hot mess and I'm not sure that they'll find Rossi any time soon. What is our next move, besides telling her that she may have to pay up for her brother?"

"Get back immediately and let us know when Rossi calls again. In the meantime, we'll split surveillance of the hotel between Tom and Paul. And we'll put Sabrina on the hunt at the pawn shops," Matt replied.

He glanced across the dark wood conference table and over at both younger men. "Tom, go home and get some sleep. Paul, go relieve Sabrina."

Both nodded, gathered their papers, and started to leave the room.

"Pay attention. My gut tells me something may break loose soon," Shawn added.

Ian glanced over at this brother, halfway expecting that there would be a repeat of yesterday's effort for him to seek out counseling. Instead Shawn stopped outside the meeting room door and waited for Ian to walk up to him.

"Everything okay with Jillian staying at your place?" Shawn asked.

"Sure. Why do you ask?"

No sooner than the words left his lips, he wished he hadn't posed the question. Of course, his brother would be worried about any 'episodes'.

Shawn crooked a small grin. "Just wondering about you and Jillian getting along. I mean, you two used to be a couple."

His brother didn't elaborate. He didn't need to. Of course, the one person in the room who would know how well the dynamics of having a female houseguest worked. Add to the fact they had been high school sweethearts, and it was only natural to wonder if Ian and Jillian would possibly reconnect.

Ian locked eyes with Shawn, hoping that his best poker face would do the trick and stop his brother from pursuing this line of talk. "No, things have been strictly on a professional level. I'll continue to work hard to ensure she is safe until the situation is over."

Ian didn't elaborate any further. There was no way he was ever going to tell his older brother that he was keenly aware of Jillian's presence. The soft sounds as she unpacked and moved in the bedroom, the sound of the water when she took a shower, and the simple fact that when she was in the room nothing else existed.

Shawn's grin faded. Ian detected a trace of disappointment in his eyes.

"Okay. Get back to the Villa and keep us in the loop if anything happens."

"Got it." Ian replied.

***

Jillian sank into her office chair, slipped her high heeled shoes off and gently rubbed her feet. She shot a quick glance at the clock on the opposite wall and noted that the wedding party would be here within an hour.

They'd arrive in street clothes, then do hair, make-up, and dress in the rooms that they had rented. The wedding planner had arrived shortly after Ian had dropped her off and hadn't stopped for more than a few minutes to chat with Jillian before checking the dressing rooms, the chapel, and the dining room. After the flowers had arrived, the centerpieces had been set and last minute adjustments had been made to the table settings, Jillian had excused herself and went to check out the progress in the kitchen.

Larry and the team were in full swing prepping the hor d'oeuvres, the ingredients for the salad, and the vegetables that would be paired with the main course, as well also preparing some alternative menus for guests with dietary restrictions.

She turned her attention back to her hands and noticed the bruise that bloomed on her wrist. Memories of last night flooded her mind. Ian had not meant to hurt her, but when he opened his eyes, he'd been lost within whatever nightmare he had been living in. Jillian had heard stories about what happened over there and she was almost positive that Ian was suffering from post-traumatic stress disorder. Whatever had happened, he had bottled it up and hidden it away from the world. But, like a genie in a bottle, it managed to get out from time to time and the results appeared disastrous in his case.

She leaned back in her chair and conjured up the face of the young man she knew in high school. The young man who had been a bundle of nerves when he had asked her to go to prom. A soft smile broke on her lips as she recalled that only after he asked and she'd accepted, did it occur to her that Ian had been hovering around her for days. She'd been clueless that he'd been waiting for a few moments when she was alone and away from her girlfriends so that he could pop the question. When she had said yes, his excitement had bubbled.

The sweet, slightly romantic young man was a far cry from the one who had escorted her around the last twenty-four hours. Strange, she'd never thought qualities like hopefulness and trust in fellow humans could be a casualty of war.

"Hi."

Jillian's eyes shot open. She smiled and gestured for Ian to come in.

"Looks like you didn't get much sleep last night. Catnapping?"

Jillian exhaled and softly laughed. "I wish. I'm afraid the only catnapping that will be done today will be done by Simon."

Ian dropped into the chair in front of her the desk. "I hear you on that one." He sighed. "Jillian, I'm going to apologize again. I'm so sorry about what happened last night. I sometimes suffer from nightmares that are so real I believe I'm back there."

"Ian, I know you didn't do it intentionally." She paused as she considered if she should continue speaking. "You just need to seek some help. To come to terms with whatever happened, find some resolution, and peace."

"You are probably right. I thought the memories would fade and things would get better. They haven't."

"So, any updates?" Jillian asked.

His gaze met hers and the corners of his mouth turned up slightly. *Yes, they have something.*

"We've found Wesley's BMW."

Jillian's heart raced and she started to slip her feet back into her shoes. "How is Wesley?"

Ian shook his head. "Jillian. Listen to me. We found the car, we haven't found your brother, yet."

If she'd been excited seconds ago, his words caused her chest to tighten so quickly that Jillian thought she might just have a heart attack. "Where?"

"It was found in one of the old hotels down on Van Buren. It doesn't look to be damaged. The hotel manager said that Wesley paid for one week's stay but he hasn't seen him. At this point we're not sure if he's telling us the truth or not. But the tech team has placed a tracking device on the car and we have someone watching for his return."

Jillian leaned forward and covered her lips with her hands. *What was going on?* She took a deep breath in an effort to release some of the tension that coiled through her. "So we wait."

"Yeah."

She looked up at Ian. She caught it, a trace of empathy and concern mirrored briefly in his eyes. There it was, a glimpse of the man she knew in high school. He's still there, but hiding behind an emotional wall as impenetrable as a Kevlar vest.

"I want to go to the hotel, to search for him so badly, but I can't. Especially not today."

"Jillian, there is not much that you can do at this point. So stay here, do what you do best and make sure that this couple has a wedding to remember. If we can, we'll head out after and go down to the hotel. But right now, there is nothing you can do and we've got this covered."

She leaned back in her chair and slid her heels back on.

"Okay," Jillian replied softly.

"Had you heard back from Rossi?" Ian asked.

"No. Nothing. Do you think there is a problem?"

"Maybe. Jillian, if you had to come up with the payment of fifty thousand, could you do it?"

Jillian stared down at the desktop. Asking that straightforward question led her to ask and then answer others in her head. She looked up and at him. "But Rossi doesn't know where to find him either. How can be we be sure if I pay they will stop searching for him and Wes will be safe?"

No sooner than the question left her lips, Jillian realized how it sounded. "It's not that I wouldn't pay to keep my brother safe. But if Rossi is a drug dealer, he has no regard for human life and pain and suffering that the drugs create. Anyone that heartless probably won't stop hunting Wesley down."

She gazed at him, trying to read the expression in his eyes and understand what he might be thinking. *Please, Ian, tell me that giving the man the money would make this all go away and keep my brother safe.*

Ian glanced down at the carpet and was silent for several seconds.

"Jillian, here is how I see it. The police think your brother stole your stuff and is on the run. When you reported that your car was vandalized, you told them about Rossi's calls. Are they aggressively looking for Rossi? I don't know. I hope they are, but I can't guarantee that they'll find him before he finds Wes. You need to prepare so that if necessary, you can act quickly. If you have funds that are tied up in investments, you might want take steps so that you can get cash quickly."

"Yes, you're probably right," Jillian whispered. "I'll need to make some phone calls."

Ian rose from his seat. "I'll give you some privacy and if you need me, I'll be in the hallway waiting."

"Thanks."

Ian closed the door as he left her office. Silence registered, then dread, as Jillian stretched across her desk and picked up the desk phone.

CHAPTER THIRTEEN

Ian stepped out into the hallway and looked both left and right. He pulled out his cell phone and checked his text messages. *Nothing.* Given the time from when the meeting broke up with Shawn and the others and now, he'd hoped there would be a few new discoveries for him to report.

Jillian deserved answers and all he and Sonoran Security has been able to come up with was some basic information on the man who hounded her for money and the location of her brother's abandoned car.

He hissed a curse as he returned the cell phone to his jacket pocket. It felt like he was back in Iraq. His mouth went as dry as chalk, and the bagel that he'd stuffed down still sat in his stomach like a rock. Ian considered heading to the kitchen to see if he could scrounge up a bottled water or even a Sprite or 7-Up.

Exactly how long does it take to call your financial advisor to arrange to cash out funds and put them into an account where cash can be drawn out at a moment's notice? Dang if he knew. He'd mustered out of the army months ago and that wasn't a career choice you took if you wanted to waltz down the road to riches.

He'd been surprised by Jillian's candor about how she came into the funds to purchase and set up this place. Her parents were hard-working people, but certainly not that flush. Jillian had dressed nicely in high school but she wasn't one of the 'rich kids'. Must have been a blessing to come into funds at a stage in life when you know what you wanted to do and knew how to do it.

Ian walked over to the window and looked into the courtyard. The view was magnificent in his opinion. The architecture was a cross of northern Italian and Spanish influence.

A young couple strolled into the courtyard, both wearing black slacks, white tuxedo-style shirts, and black cummerbunds. The woman's dark hair had been pulled into a bun and they both carried matching black vests. A few minutes later, another man arrived, followed by others. He glanced at his wristwatch and considered if he should knock on the door and let Jillian know the wait staff was filtering in.

As if on cue, Jillian emerged from her office. The blush and lipstick she had added hid the pale, tired look on her face.

"Okay?" he asked.

"It's done. They're selling some investments, and I should have the money in my bank account in a couple of days. If Rossi wants cash, then I will have to go to the bank to get the money.

"If it gets to that, the police will certainly be involved in an effort to catch this guy," Ian said.

She shook her head slightly. "I halfway expected that I would have heard from him by now. Yet…" Jillian didn't finish the sentence. She swept her hand up to her eyes and wiped them. Taking a deep breath, she looked into the courtyard. "You know, the not knowing is the hardest part."

"Yeah," Ian whispered. "I know exactly what you mean. The fear and anticipation can eat you alive."

Jillian trained her gaze on him. She studied his face. Ian felt she'd read his mind and picked up on his reference to Iraq. Seconds passed as the silence between then yawned. She cracked a soft smile. "Sorry for the meltdown last night."

"You didn't exactly lose it and besides I liked where things led," Ian replied.

"I could really use a hug."

Jillian had dropped that as a quiet, casual comment. Ian reached out and touched her arm to stop her from walking away. She paused and then in seconds, stepped closer and into his arms. She wrapped her arms around his waist and tightened them, drawing closer as she laid her head on his chest.

The move was so seamless that Ian almost didn't remember opening his arms to draw her in. She smelled of light perfume, and the sunlight filtering through the trees in the courtyard and the window gave delicate streaks of golden-red highlights to her hair. For the first time in as long as he could remember, the emotional ice that he felt entombed in fractured and warmth fingered its way in.

He exhaled as Jillian pulled back slightly and gazed up at him for a few seconds. The corners of her mouth tipped up and then she stood on her toes and kissed him. Her lips were gentle and sweet, and she'd taken him off guard. He barely responded before she pulled back.

Jillian placed her fingers to her lips, drew in a deep breath, and exhaled, before stepping back out of his embrace. "Oops, I guess I shouldn't have done…"

No way was he going to let her apologize for taking the first step. This was by far the best thing that had happened in months--no, scratch that--years. He grasped her as if he didn't, she'd disappear in thin air. "No. Don't apologize."

A flush bloomed in her cheeks and he cupped her face. He leaned over and kissed her back.

She eased into his embrace and wrapped her arms around his shoulders. Her arms tightened as if she needed to hold on to him for dear life.

Someone cleared their throat, followed by silence, and then a cough. *Oh crap! Yep, Jillian's worst nightmare had just happened.* Opening his eyes, he loosened his grip and stepped back a step. Jillian did the same and caught what must have been a sheepish look on his face.

Ian glanced over at the wedding planner, then back at Jillian. He rolled his eyes back to the woman and nodded in her direction. Jillian's mouth opened slightly. Jillian responded by straightening and turning to face the planner. "Yes, is there anything we can do?"

The woman flashed a Cheshire cat smile at Ian, then redirected her gaze at Jillian. "I've received a text message. The bridal party is about ten minutes out from arrival."

Jillian nodded. "The dressing rooms are ready. Do you want me to help you escort everyone?"

The planner nodded. "I'd appreciate that."

Jillian turned to him. "We'll talk later."

"I'd like to head to the kitchen and pick up a bottled water," Ian replied.

The wedding planner snorted a soft laugh. "Might be a good idea."

Ian watched the pair walk away. He raked his hand through his hair. So much for the discretion that Jillian was trying to maintain. If the wedding planner talked about this, the news would spread through the employees like wildfire.

Jillian would be upset, and he knew why. It was a chain of command thing where the personal activities of your supervisors were generally not up for discussion. Gossip and speculation eroded authority, and the rank and file were distracted at a time when the result could be deadly.

At least in the civilian world, gossip wasn't fatal. Ian glanced down the hallway. Both women were out of sight. Jillian might regret it if word got out about them. He smiled. But, God help him, he wasn't.

Ian's smart phone vibrated and he pulled it out of his pocket. Matt's number showed and he picked up the call. "What's happened?"

"Has Ms. Connors heard from Rossi?"

"No," Ian answered. "She made a few phone calls to free up cash in case it would be needed. Anything new on your end?"

"Yes, and Ms. Connors isn't going to like it."

CHAPTER FOURTEEN

Lord give me patience and deliver me from bridezillas, Jillian prayed in earnest silence. In the scheme of things, what she asked was probably irreverent, but honestly right now she meant it.

She stood in silence as the young woman stood in the center of the room with her bridesmaids and mother buzzing around her like she was a queen bee. On the surface, the woman appeared to be nice and pleasant, but Jillian noticed the change in demeanor as she assessed the dressing room, the beverages, and tray of finger sandwiches, as well as the floral arrangements. Jillian had seen this before. This bride had allowed her wedding to become less about a marriage and more of a media event held in her honor.

Jillian stood silently as the wedding planner stepped away, poured a small glass of champagne, and served it to the bride, who sat in front of a mirror as her stylist put the finishing touches on her make-up and hairstyle.

The words from the ceremony rolled through her mind. *For richer or poorer, in sickness and health, till death do us part.* When those challenges came, would this woman go the distance? Jillian tamped down the questions. It wasn't her place to play marriage counselor. Her role was to provide the bride with the best location for the wedding and hope and pray that her instincts regarding this bride and her marriage were incorrect.

She forced a smile and addressed the group. "Is there anything else that I can provide or be of assistance with?" The wedding planner looked over at her and gently tapped the bride on the shoulder. The young woman turned and studied Jillian, who deliberately brightened her smile.

"No. We're fine," the bride replied before raising the champagne glass to her lips for another sip.

"Good. If you need anything, please notify us." With that comment, Jillian left the room. As she closed the door behind her, she shook her head. Usually this type of behavior didn't bother her, but for some reason, today she was struggling to find patience with it all. Clearly, all the unanswered questions and uncertainty were wearing her down.

"Jillian. We've got some news to report."

At the sound of Ian's voice, she turned. In the seconds it took for him to walk up to her, she studied his body language and facial expression, hoping for a clue as to what she was about to hear.

"Tell me," she ordered quietly.

"We've found one of the TV's you've reported missing. It's at a pawn shop. There may be more there."

She swallowed and nodded, trying to purposefully remain calm. "Where's the shop?"

"In central Phoenix. I know you can't leave right now, but I would like to have you come with me to check this out as soon as you can."

"I won't be able to leave for several hours. With the wedding and reception…"

"I know," Ian responded before she could finish off her sentence. "These types of places stay open till late in the evening. So if at all possible, I would like to check this out tonight."

"Okay," Jillian replied. "I have to do one more final walk-through right now." She turned and started to walk down the hallway toward the banquet room and chapel. Numbness filtered through her. Her legs turned stiff and clumsy and the spacious hallway seemed to close in on her.

"Jillian?"

She turned back to look at Ian. His face was etched with concern. He closed the distance to her and grasped her arm.

Jillian took a step back and raised her hand as if to ward him off. "I'm fine."

"From the looks of things, I doubt that. Here."

Ian guided her to a bench on the left side of the hallway. "Come sit down. You look like you've seen a ghost."

As she sank down on the seat, her mind began to race, as if a floodgate had been opened and a million questions rushed in, all asking to be answered at the same time. Ian stood nearby, almost protectively. His smart phone must have buzzed because he retrieved it from his coat and looked at it for a few moments.

"They've found more," he said. "Sabrina has spoken to the shop manager. It looks like Wesley signed the paperwork."

She glanced up from the tile on the floor and focused on the wall across the hallway in front of her. Strange, every time the subject had come up within the last few days, she'd been on the brink of tears. Now, nothing. No watery eyes, no battling back the urge to cry, just numbness. The police had been correct; her brother had taken everything.

"I just wish I knew why."

She glanced up at Ian. He didn't reply. For the past couple of days he'd been asking questions that she refused to even consider the possible answers. Now, it looked like what the police and Ian had suggested had happened.

She sighed. "How late?"

Ian looked up from his phone. "What?"

"How late is the pawn shop open?"

"I'll check." He then began to type on his cell phone.

Jillian shook her head. "I don't have someone who I can delegate supervising this event to so I can't leave now."

Ian snorted softly. "No worries. They're open twenty-four hours."

"Figures." She turned her head and watched as the groom and his best man entered through the front gate and into the court-yard. "Ah, the lucky man arrives."

Ian shot her a glance. "You don't sound too sure about that."

"Call it women's intuition or simply my ability to read brides, but I think the future for this couple will be interesting. Excuse me. I need to get the gentlemen to their ready room."

***

Ian stepped back a step as she strode off to the young men.

Part of him was curious as to what Jillian saw when she read this bride. But maybe it was better that he did not know. He looked down as the text from Sabrina. *Found more at Central Pawn. Shop owners sort of cooperative. Saw paperwork and seller name is Wesley Connors. Do you want me to contact Phx PD?*

Ian texted back. *Will get back to you on this. Thanks.* He placed the cell phone back into his jacket pocket and looked around. There wasn't much he could do except make a concerted effort to be out of everyone's way for the next few hours. The question was, where should he hide out?

***

Ian popped his head through the doors to the kitchen. He'd expected that things would be a bit crazy with Larry dashing around and barking orders to the team of cooks. Instead it was quiet, with the guys leaning against the counters and a large number of plates lined up with military precision waiting to have food placed on them.

"Sorry to intrude, but is it possible that I could get a bottled water?"

Larry looked over. "Sure."

The chef gestured for Ian to join them, and, as he approached the group of men, one broke off and returned with a water bottle and handed it to him. Ian unscrewed the cap and took several large gulps.

One of the cooks spoke. "Need another?"

Ian shook his head. "No, I'm good. Thanks." He surveyed the room. "Somehow I thought you would be running around."

Larry grinned and threw a knowing glance at the other cooks.

"That only happens with those cooking competition shows. Appetizers and salads are ready to go and just need to be plated, and we'll start the meat and vegetables around the middle to end of the wedding service. That will go quickly."

"The wedding cake?"

"Already set up in the ballroom with the display," replied one of the three cooks.

"I'm impressed," Ian replied, and then nodded at Larry. "How long have you worked here?"

"Me? About four years. Abe and Tony have been here a little over two, and Eric is the newcomer. He's been here a little over a year."

Ian reflected that the team was relatively new. But then, he hadn't asked Jillian how long La Villa de Gardena had been open for business. He grinned and hoped his next question didn't sound too suspicious. "What did you do before you came here?"

Larry waved a hand at his team. "We're a diverse group. I was an army cook. After I got out, I worked in a number of places before this opportunity came along. Abe worked his way up the ladder at a couple of franchise restaurants. Tony, he's the 'properly trained' chef. Went to a cooking school. The Phoenix Culinary Academy, right?"

The young man with dark hair and even darker eyes nodded.

"Eric worked over at the Phoenician for a while," Larry added.

"I can see Jillian has put together an experienced team." And he meant what he said. Each man possessed a relaxed and confident air about him, with the exception of Eric, who looked very young, inexperienced, and just a little anxious. The Phoenician was a very prestigious resort. Not that working here was bad, but in the scheme of things, this was probably a step down for Eric, and for a second he wondered why the young man would have left his former employer.

"As far as hospitality goes, this is a great job and we're all glad to be here," Abe chimed in. "Yes, we have some crunch time when an event takes place, but overall we aren't putting in the hours you normally would if you're working in a restaurant."

Larry grinned. "And Abe and his wife just had a baby earlier this year. He enjoys having time with his family."

"Sounds great to me," Ian acknowledged.

He'd not thought that this type of job provided some quality of life time. Ian finished off the bottle and screwed the top back on. *Quality of life, what a novel concept. Maybe someday I'll know what that is.*

Ian tossed the empty bottle in the blue recycle container by the door.

Jillian popped through the door. "Larry, are you ready for the walk-through with the wait staff?"

"Yep, are they all here?" the chef responded.

"They're in the banquet room. Let's get them debriefed."

She turned and headed back through the kitchen door, the head chef on her heels. Ian glanced over at the remaining cooks. Should he follow them or stay here? Abe gestured to the door. "If you don't leave, we'll put you to work. Things are about to get very busy soon."

Ian crooked a grin at the man and turned to catch up with Jillian and her head chef. By the time he'd caught up with them, the pair had assembled the wait staff in a half circle and began to go over the menu and the sequence of when the courses were served and which other accessory or secondary food items came with each course. He hung back at the wall near the door and listened as questions were answered and the clear course of directions were given.

He had to give it to Jillian. Larry knew his stuff and his background as a military chef showed with his precision on timelines and firm direction on what the wait staff was expected to do.

His phone buzzed in his coat pocket. Ian retrieved it and looked at the message. *Found more. A stereo unit and some jewelry. Manager stated when he bought them from Wesley, they had not been reported as stolen. Now nervous that he'll have to surrender them and lose the money he spent for them. Should I call Phx PD?*

Ian looked over at Jillian. He texted back. *Not yet.*

CHAPTER FIFTEEN

Ian opened the door to the pawn shop. Jillian entered, took a few steps, then stopped and waited until he reached her side. "Never been to a pawn shop before. Have you?"

He considered for a few seconds whether her question was genuine or simply a nervous conversation starter, before replying, "No."

"Is there anyone special we should talk to?"

"Sabrina texted that we should ask for the manager. She says his name is Croft."

He'd halfway expected that the place would be dark, musty, and cluttered with junk. However, the items appeared to be merchandised in general categories. A saxophone, trumpet, and some large amps along with a few electrical guitars made him conclude they were looking at the musical instrument section.

Jillian stopped by a well-worn violin and she stroked it gently with her fingers. He stilled and touched her shoulder. "Anything look familiar?"

She turned and forced a weak smile. "No."

Ian pointed to the counter that ran the length of the back of the showroom. The man who stood behind it appeared to be arranging jewelry in a glass display case. He gestured to the counter. "Let's go."

Jillian's lips pressed together and worry flashed in her eyes. "Okay. No guts, no glory, right?"

Her choice of words caused him to wince. She couldn't have known but he'd seen his share of guts and there certainly was no glory to it. Not by any stretch of the imagination. Jillian must have taken his silence as her cue to lead the way through shelves filled with a wide array of instruments that even contained an accordion on the way to the man. She ambled slowly as she surveyed the merchandise on the shelves.

The man left the counter to stand directly in front of the aisle they were in. "Can I help you?"

Jillian trained her gaze at the man. She plucked at the strap of her purse. "Yes, I hope so. My name is Jillian Connors and this is Ian Randall. Earlier this afternoon, a work associate of Mr. Randall was in here and reported that you have some merchandise that had been removed from my home."

The man, short, stocky and with a receding hairline wrinkled his nose. "You work with Sabrina?"

"Yes."

Now it appeared to be the man's turn to look nervous. He gestured for them to approach the counter. "Well, Mr. Randall, as I told your associate this afternoon, we have to check all merchandise presented for sale or loan against a list in national database to determine if the item has been reported as stolen before we will buy or loan against it. Then any item we acquire is put on a thirty-day hold before we can actually put the item on the floor for sale."

The man gestured to Ian and Jillian to follow him down the length of the display case to the cash register. "Kind of thought that you would have been here earlier this evening."

Ian spied a wall clock next to the register. Already close to nine-twenty.

"I had clients. I would've come earlier if I could have," Jillian said.

"Are you Croft?" Ian asked.

"Nope. I'm Bill Drummond."

Jillian spoke. "I'm still having a hard time believing that Wesley pawned my things."

Drummond looked at her and Ian couldn't figure out what the man was thinking. Generally, Ian could read people well. It was a useful tool when trying to survive in a war zone. Even on the other side of the world, a person's facial expression and body language were easy to read. Drummond, he decided, gave away nothing. He regarded Jillian with cool, expressionless eyes.

"Have you ever done business with a pawn shop before?"

Jillian shook her head. "No."

"Okay, let me tell you how this works. When someone comes into a pawn shop, they can get money for their possessions either by taking a loan or by selling the item outright. The advantage is that if one needs to raise funds quick, or if you have poor credit or even no credit, we can be a good option for many folks. Don't get me wrong. This isn't a non-profit organization. We do not pay full price for your items, because if you don't come back and pay off your loan, or if we resell our stuff, we need to make a profit."

Jillian nodded. "So what about people who take things which belong to others and sell them?"

A smile broke on the pawnbroker's face. "Great question. We take precautions. First we require picture identification of the person selling and we run the serial numbers in a database to check to see that they haven't been reported as stolen."

Drummond walked over to the cash register and pulled out some papers. "At the time that…" The man paused as he glanced down and read from the papers in his hand. "When Wesley Connor sold the items, the serial numbers did not come up in the database."

The pawn broker looked at Jillian. "When did you report them as stolen?"

"I turned in the paperwork to the Phoenix police department two days ago."

Drummond frowned. "Well, it looks like he walked through our doors almost 24 hours before you turned in your list to the police department. The good news for you is that we still have them. It's in the back storage for that thirty-day hold. The police will take the items as evidence, and when the case has been closed and Wesley is duly punished for stealing and selling your items, you'll get the stuff back."

"What happens for you?" Jillian asked.

"We lose out. We accidentally purchased stolen property. We're out the money and the merchandise."

Jillian looked at Ian. He could see the indecision in her eyes as she mulled over what to do next.

She surveyed all the items in the shop. "But it wasn't your fault. You followed the protocol and you got hurt because of it."

Drummond said nothing. Ian studied the pawnbroker's poker face and wondered what his thoughts on the matter were. The man appeared to be a decent guy, but he stood to lose money on this deal now that the goods were found as stolen.

"How much?" Jillian asked.

The older man studied the paperwork in his hands. "All told, around $1700."

Jillian set her purse firmly on the glass showcase and extended her hand. "May I see the paperwork?"

Drummond handed the papers over to her. Ian walked over and glanced over Jillian's shoulder as they read the documents. Wesley's driver's license was on the top sheet of the stack of papers and his photo had shown that he'd matured since he'd last seen her brother. Jillian flipped through the pages, they had the large flat screen television and other electronic items. On the last page, she gasped and glanced up to Ian. "My grandmother's pearl broach. Wesley took her broach. I didn't even notice that the broach was missing."

Her hand rose to her lips as she handed the paperwork back to Drummond. "He took her broach and I missed that," she whispered. "Ian, what should I do?"

"You need to let the police department know you've found some of your stolen items. They'll secure them."

He'd expected her to cry. She'd been on the verge so many times over the past few days. Instead, she was calm, collected, and dry-eyed.

A determined look settled into her eyes. "I can't do that.

What would my parents and sister say? I press charges and put my brother in jail? They'd be furious with me for doing that."

"Jillian, so you're telling me that they would expect you to take the hit for Wesley stealing your things and to let him walk off scot-free?" he asked in disbelief.

"No." She bit the word out. "They'll say I deserved this. Something they've been holding back from saying for a while now."

"What?" He glanced over at the pawn broker, who watched the exchange without any comment or readable expression on his face.

"We need a little privacy to talk," Ian growled at the man.

An electronic doorbell chimed and a couple walked through the front door.

Drummond grunted. "I'm not going anywhere. You and the lady can talk in the corner of the store or step outside."

"Fine," Ian said.

"You pick."

She pointed her finger to the far front corner of the showroom. "There."

Jillian marched to the other end of the room with Ian following closely. They'd barely reached the corner before Ian countered, "How could they say that you deserved this?"

Jillian spun around. "Because I was supposed to watch him. To make sure he didn't relapse. I failed."

She stopped, threaded her hand through her hair, and glanced around the showroom.

She leaned in closer and whispered, "Don't you see, they expected me to see this coming and stop things before they got out of hand. I didn't. As you so aptly pointed out a day ago, I had no idea who his favorite sports team was. I wasn't aware Wesley was on thin ice with his employer. I was clueless. They'll blame me."

"Well, that's stupid," Ian retorted.

"That may be, but…."

"But nothing. Let me tell you a couple of things, and I'm happy to tell your family, who appear all too ready to dump the blame and responsibility on to you, that drug addicts are very good at hiding their problem until it's out of control. Believe me, I've seen that firsthand. The loneliness, isolation, and not to mention you're constantly thinking someone wants you dead. It'll get to you over time. Wesley isn't the only one looking to drugs as a way to escape."

At his words, Jillian's eyes softened and whispered. "Ian. You?"

He shook his head vigorously. "No, I never did drugs. But I saw it. And, for what it's worth, relapsing is more common than permanently kicking the habit. Ultimately, you have to deal with what pushed you there in the first place. If you don't, even if you stop, you'll start again."

Jillian opened her mouth as if to reply, and then closed it. She took a deep breath and closed her eyes. She exhaled and whispered, "Okay."

"Okay, what?"

Her gaze lighted on the small domed black orb on the ceiling which housed a security camera.

"What are you going to do?"

CHAPTER SIXTEEN

He's right. Jillian bit her lower lip, took a slow deep breath, and stared out the passenger window. When Wesley first moved in, she had stepped into the mode of regularly asking her younger brother where he was going, who he was with, and what he planned to do. Whether it was out of fear, concern, or as some level of belief that if she knew what Wesley did twenty-four hours a day, she could prevent a relapse, she couldn't say. However, the more she tried to keep tabs on Wesley, the more elusive he became.

It finally had come to a head one night when he'd exploded at her. "You're not my mother, and I'm not a child anymore, so quit trying to run my life and get one for yourself."

Her brother's words had stung. What was hardest to accept was the truth of what he'd said. Wesley was correct. He was a grown man and would have to be responsible for his life. Worse, the comment that she needed to get one herself had hurt even more.

Had she failed to, as her brother put it, "get a life"?   On the surface, it appeared she had one. A good one. She had her business, but on a personal level, she'd put life on hold.

Jillian told herself her primary focus was to grow the business to the point it was a profitable venture. Lord knows, she had invested her entire inheritance into it. If it failed, she'd be broke. Putting her love life on pause made sense.

The problem was her personal life had been on pause for years. That didn't make sense. Of course, she'd dated on an off over the years, but there had been no long term, or exclusive relationships. Ian's return to the U.S. and his presence on this case had brought that buried fact to the light of day.

She glanced over to the driver's side and looked at Ian in the semi-darkness of the car. What about him? Did he have anyone special?

He'd not mentioned anyone. There were no photos or hints if one were to judge by his apartment. She sighed. It wasn't any of her business. But, it could be. They'd kissed twice in the last twenty-four hours. Ian Randall wouldn't step out on a girlfriend. Commitment and fidelity were important to him.

"A penny for your thoughts," Ian said.

"Just thinking about a lot of things," Jillian replied.

"Still mulling over whether to inform the P.D.?"

"No. I'm mulling over other stuff. In regards to the stuff Wesley sold, I'm going to take a day to consider what the next step should be."

Ian didn't comment. He didn't have to. Jillian knew he felt she should let the police department know that some of the missing items had been located. She returned her gaze to the view out the car window. As they drove east down the 101 freeway, the city lights twinkled up into the foothills of the mountains.

"I have a question for you," Jillian said.

"Oh, what?"

"In the pawn shop, you talked about seeing people use drugs for an escape. How bad was it?"

The seconds ticked by and Ian didn't reply. Jillian turned and gazed at his silhouette in the darkness of the car. She sensed her question had touched a raw, emotional nerve.

Ian sighed. "It was bad."

The emotions he described in the pawn shop when he spoke to what drove people to drugs floated in her mind. Loneliness, isolation, and constant fear. She could understand that. Maybe not on a gut level, but at least intellectually.

"How bad?"

"I saw my friends get maimed and some of them died." Ian's voice was dull and weary.

Jillian leaned her head against the headrest, and she closed her eyes. "No wonder you have nightmares."

"Yeah. I know how you feel when you say that you feel responsible. At times, the guilt and fear comes out of nowhere, hits so hard that I believe I'm about to have a nervous breakdown. Why did it happen to them and not me?" He stopped speaking and weariness descended upon the space like a cold, wet blanket. "How come I'm back home in one piece and alive when others weren't so lucky? I play the events over and over in my head and ask, could I have done something different? Would it have mattered? Every time I ask, I get nothing. No answers."

Ian had a point. It wasn't the questions that drove you nuts, it was the lack of answers. She could beat herself up with all the things she could or should have done in regards to her brother's drug recovery. But, if Ian was right? What if she had spent twenty-four hours a day watching her brother? Would it have made a difference?

Now his comments in the pawn shop made sense. Ian pushed for reporting the finds to the police. Yes, Wesley, if and when he was caught, would have to deal with the legal consequences, but maybe what it would take was hitting bottom before he'd come to terms with his issues. The problem was, would her family back her on this issue or would they rally to rescue and protect her brother? Jillian's hand rose and she rubbed her forehead.

"I can't deal with this tonight. I'm fried and need a good night's sleep and a clear head before I make this decision."

"Makes sense. Since you're so concerned about the family's reaction, it may be time to give them an update and talk to them about what to do next."

"You're probably right," Jillian replied. It was time to lay the facts candidly on the table so everybody knew what had happened. "Rossi. How do I explain Rossi to them? They're going to have a lot of questions regarding the demand for fifty thousand and frankly, I don't have much in terms of answers."

"Just level with them. Tell them what you know. It's time that they get a full briefing on things. If you don't know, tell them that. They need to be in the loop as to what's going on."

"My sister already knows most of it. But my parents don't know about Rossi and Wesley clearing out his trust account," Jillian said softly. This would be an ugly conversation.

Ian took the exit ramp and slowed. "Good news is that I'm betting Simon will be very happy to see you."

Jillian laughed softly. "Probably will be. Consider yourself warned. Siamese cats are very vocal."

"Duly noted."

For the next few minutes as they drove to Ian's apartment, neither of them spoke thanks to just plain out-and-out exhaustion. As she predicted, Simon met them at the door, meowing and curling and rubbing himself around their legs.

Ian set his keys and cell phone on the counter between the kitchen and dining area and then walked to the bedroom. "Let me get my stuff out and then you can take a shower."

Jillian scooped up Simon. The cat purred loudly as she softly scratched all his favorite spots.

Ian's cell phone rang. As the second ring chimed, Jillian walked over to it. "Ian, your phone is ringing."

She glanced at the phone's screen. The name Thomas showed. "I think it's someone from the agency."

On the third ring, Ian rounded the corner. Jillian picked up the device and handed it to him. "Here."

Ian swiped the screen and answered, "Yeah."

Surprise registered on his face. "Say again?"

He turned and looked at Jillian. "Okay, track it and give us an update where it's going. We're coming."

Ian disconnected the call. "You may want to change into some jeans and comfortable shoes and fast."

Jillian set the cat down and swallowed. "What happened?"

"Someone just came to the hotel and picked up your brother's BMW."

Chapter Seventeen

Jillian leaned forward in the passenger seat and scanned the blue-collar neighborhood, hoping to view her brother's BMW. A young man, who looked to be in his middle twenties, stepped out of the darkness, into the headlights and approached their car.

"That's Thomas," Ian said.

She swallowed. Why had she not bothered to bring a bottle of water of something? Her mouth felt as dry as chalk.

"He doesn't look happy," she muttered.

"No, he doesn't." Ian replied as he pulled the car over to the right curb and behind the young man's pick-up truck.

Thomas walked up to the driver's side door and Ian rolled down the window.

"Nice night for a drive," Thomas said quietly.

"Right," Ian replied. "Okay, give us the details."

Thomas glanced over at Jillian and nodded a silent greeting.

"Well, we found the car at that hotel on Van Buren. The hotel clerk wasn't exactly the most cooperative about giving us information as to where Wesley was. The only thing he said was that your brother had paid for a week in advance. If what the hotel clerk had said was accurate, then it would pay off to case the place and see if Wesley would return. Just in case we missed him, Matt had us place a tracking device on the vehicle. About an hour and half ago, this guy shows up, pulls out the key fob, unlocks the car, and drives it off."

"So he didn't hotwire the car?" Jillian asked.

"Would be hard to do," Thomas replied.

"Luxury automobiles tend to have alarms and security systems on them to prevent the vehicles from being stolen," Ian added.

Jillian nodded. "You're right. Had he tried to break into the car, the alarms would have been triggered."

"For what it's worth, they guy drove the car sensibly," Thomas said. "Oh, I did call Matt and he's on his way."

The cell phone chimed. Thomas stepped back from the car door and checked the screen. "Paul and Sabrina are coming. They should be here soon. Matt texted that we're not to approach the house until reinforcements arrive."

"Fine," Ian replied.

Jillian leaned back in the passenger seat and watched Thomas trot back to his truck. *Reinforcements?* The word summoned up the image of anticipated battle and her stomach tightened into a knot. *Is that what we're going to be doing? Going into battle?*

"Ian, do you think this guy knows where Wesley is?"

He trained his gaze on her. She couldn't see his face clearly in the darkness of the car's interior.

"I'm not sure, Jilli."

She bit her lower lip, glanced down at her phone and noted the time. It was approaching one a.m. Ian laid his hand over hers. "We should know more soon."

"I hope so. This not knowing is driving me crazy."

Jillian took in a deep breath and closed her eyes. Normally, she'd be back at home, sleeping soundly. Just how much longer could she go without eventually hitting a wall physically?

Ian shifted in his seat and Jillian opened her eyes. A vehicle pulled up behind them. Light flooded the car interior and then disappeared as the large truck turned off the lights.

"Stay inside the car," Ian ordered.

Jillian twisted in her seat to peer into the back window as a man stepped out of the truck and walked toward them. "Matt?"

"Yep," Ian replied as he opened the driver's door, stepped out, and walked toward the man. Within seconds, Thomas reappeared to join them.

The three men huddled below the pale light from a street light. Matt must have said something Ian didn't like, because Ian's posture went rigid and he shook his head.

What is going on? Jillian strained around the headrest and hoped that perhaps she could hear more of the conversation.

"This is ridiculous," she muttered. "Why am I sitting here in the car while "the men" decide what to do next? For pity's sake, it's my brother that's missing. It's his car they followed. I should have a say in what to do next."

Irritation bubbled into anger as she continued to watch the men as they continued to talk. "That's it. I've had enough."

She unfastened her seat belt, opened the car door, and

slammed it. The three men in unison stopped talking and watched her stride up to them.

"What's the game plan?" As she got closer, she could see the expressions on their faces. Thomas' brow creased in worry, while a knowing smirk lifted Ian's lips. He took a step back, providing her the space to join the team.

Matt studied her quietly. Jillian tried reading him and getting a handle on what he felt about all of this, but the tall sandy-haired man was as inscrutable as the sphinx.

Thomas spoke first. "We're hashing out the next steps."

"Okay."

"We have a couple problems we need to address," Matt said.

"And they are?"

"First, the car hasn't technically been reported stolen. Second, it's one in the morning. If we want some degree of cooperation from this guy, I don't think that pounding on his door at this hour is going to get that. If it were me, I wouldn't answer the door, would you?"

Jillian crossed her arms. "Maybe. Maybe not. So are you proposing that we all sit her for the next few hours and do what? Wait till he steps out to pick up the newspaper in his driveway?"

"Jillian…"

"I don't believe this. You're behaving as if you're scared of this guy. He's got my brother's car. He may know where my brother is. You want me to just sit here and wait?" She threaded her hand through her hair. "I've had enough of this. I'll go."

"No, wait," Ian ordered.

Jillian spun around and stared at him. "What?"

He took a couple of steps toward her. As he neared, Jillian

became keenly aware that he towered a good six to seven inches over her. "Have you ever been shot?"

She paused. *Where did that question come from?* "No."

"I think you need to consider the following before you make a move. One, we don't know who we're dealing with here. Your brother owes money to a man who has a history of dealing in drugs. Your brother was a drug addict and may be one again. If we go pounding on a door at this hour, and if this guy is affiliated with Rossi, it's likely he's armed. Anyone who cares so little for human life that they would traffic in drugs probably will have no problem shooting someone."

Jillian gulped. "I need to find Wesley."

"I know," Ian replied. "But let's not get anyone killed in the process. We almost lost Shawn when he was shot on assignment, and for what it's worth, I've seen enough carnage to last me a lifetime."

He extended his hand. "Come back and let's sort this out."

Jillian glanced past Ian to Matt and Thomas.

"You're concerned, tired, and hanging on by your last frayed nerve. They get it," Ian whispered to her.

Jillian crossed her arms across her chest to prevent Ian from taking her hand. Ian took a step toward the other two men and then stopped.

"Okay," Jillian whispered and she joined him and retraced the few yards she'd traveled seconds ago. Down the street, a pair of headlights appeared. Everyone moved closer to the parked cars and watched the car get closer.

The dark, late model import sedan slowed down as it neared the group and then pulled over. The person behind the wheel turned off the lights and engine. Within seconds, a young woman and man appeared and joined the group.

"Jillian, meet Sabrina and Paul." Ian whispered.

The young couple nodded a greeting. Jillian studied Sabrina and after few seconds, forced a smile. *Well, what do you know, there is at least one other woman on this team. Thank goodness.*

Sabrina returned the smile while her eyes held a knowing expression.

Matt updated the new arrivals as to what had happened. Jillian watched the team's expressions as he recapped the options. *They are so young*, she thought. The realization struck her. She considered herself to be young. Heck, she was almost in her thirties, but in the face of three employees that were probably close to a decade younger, she felt a pang in her gut. *Where had the time gone?* It seemed like it was just a couple years ago when she had graduated from college and started on her first job.

Jillian glanced over at Ian. His attention was focused on Matt. *My goodness, Ian, has it been that long? Look at who we are today.* As if he sensed being watched, Ian looked over and met her gaze.

"Okay, now that you two are up to speed, I'm open to suggestions," Matt finished.

Jillian shifted her focus to the team.

Silence followed, and Jillian heard a cat issue an angry meow from a nearby house. Sabrina cleared her throat and spoke. "I agree that if we all show up as a group on this man's doorstep it's likely to get ugly quick. I know this area, and this guy, if we're lucky might call the police, if we're not he may decide to handle things himself."

Jillian swallowed. Ian had startled her when he'd asked her if she'd ever been shot. In the minutes that followed since their talk, she had wondered if he had said that to get her attention. Now, when Sabrina also suggested the same possibility, a slight adrenaline buzz began to hum through her.

Sabrina shot her a sober glance. "Your brother, between the pawn shop, the hotel location, and this neighborhood, is operating in some rough and dangerous places."

Jillian couldn't find any words to respond to the young woman's comment.

"I'm suggesting that Jillian and I go speak with this guy."

The response from the men on the team was unified. Heads shook, arms crossed chests, and Thomas muttered a curse.

"I don't think that's a good idea to send the two of you in," Paul added quietly.

"I do," Sabrina replied. "Let me explain why. Jillian and I are not as intimidating when compared to all of you showing up on the doorstep as a gang." The woman emphasized the word gang as she spoke it.

"I'd like to remind you that we're in the heart of gang territory. Many of the people who live in the neighborhood have family members who are members of a gang or know someone who is a member. Let's face facts, if Jillian and I are on their doorstep, we're two women. They will be curious and likely to open the door. If two guys are knocking at the door…" Sabrina didn't finish her statement. She didn't need to.

Jillian knew what the woman hinted at. There wasn't a week that went by where on the local evening news a shooting wasn't reported. More importantly, she'd be in face-to-face contact with the man who had her brother's car. Maybe he would talk to her.

"I agree," she added.

All the men trained their gaze on her.

Sabrina checked her phone. "It's almost 2 a.m."

"Okay, let's go."

Matt exhaled. "I don't like this, but I think it's our best option. Just a few words. One, do not go into the house. Not for any reason. Stay where we can see you. Second, if the guy gets combative, don't push it. Back off and leave. Got it?"

"Yes," Jillian replied.

"I'll get back in my car since I'm the closest and can watch you two without being seen," Thomas said.

"The rest of you need to get in your cars and pull back. You don't want anyone seeing a cluster of unfamiliar cars and assume the worst," Sabrina added.

The young Hispanic woman glanced over to Jillian. "You ready?"

"Yes." Jillian was surprised how calm she sounded. The light adrenaline charge had amped up considerably in the late minute.

The two of them stood on the side of the street as the men melted away from the group and began to move the cars back away from the residence. Ian drove his sedan down the street and stopped around six houses down. When the only vehicle nearby was Thomas', Sabrina touched her upper arm. "Let's do this."

CHAPTER EIGHTEEN

As the two of them walked closer to the front porch of the house, Jillian's heart pounded and her senses heightened. The light floral scent of orange tree blossoms floated on the air. Strange, she hadn't noticed that before now.

Her feet registered the soft, almost imperceptible give of the asphalt, punctuated by the occasional soft bump of a small pebble.

"Do you speak Spanish?"

"What?" Jillian replied.

"Habla espanol?" Sabrina asked quietly.

"No."

"If he starts speaking in Spanish, let me talk with him."

The two walked to the front porch. No porch light, and both of them were in full shadow.

"Ring the bell. When someone answers, introduce yourself. Be humble. Act worried. You're looking for your brother."

Jillian fought back the impulse to snort out a laugh. *Worried? You have no idea how worried I am.* She pushed the button for the doorbell and heard the tones echo through the house followed by silence. She counted to ten and reached for the button again, when Sabrina gently caught her wrist. Seconds later, the porch lights came on.

Jillian gulped while her heart seemed to pound so rapidly that it felt like she was running a race. The soft click of a lock turning caught her attention, and then the door opened slightly and a man stared back from the dark interior of the house.

"Yes?" He asked with a voice fuzzy with sleep.

"Hi, my name is Jillian Connors, and if I could have a few minutes of your time, I would like to ask you a few questions."

She blinked. Had she just said that? It sounded like she was some telephone survey taker. If someone had said that to her after knocking on her door at this hour of the morning, she would have slammed the door in their face.

The man rubbed his face. "What? Who are you? Do you know what time it is?"

With each successive question, his voice became increasingly awake and agitated.

Jillian took a step forward and when she caught the man's irritated glare, she backed up. "I'm sorry for disturbing you, but this is important. My brother's missing and his car's parked in your driveway. Do you know where he is? Have you seen him?"

The man blinked and anger burned in his eyes. "I don't know your brother. I bought the car this afternoon. It was legal. Leave. Now. Or I'll call the police."

"No, please. Just another second," Jillian pleaded. "My brother disappeared just over two days ago. I think he's in trouble. I'm just trying to find him, to help. I'm sorry I woke you up. But it's important. I don't care about the car. I'm just trying to find my brother."

The man stared at her for a few seconds. From what she could discern, the anger had dialed back a couple notches, but his expression was still very guarded.

"Who's there?" A woman's voice came from behind the man, and he glanced over his shoulder to speak to her in Spanish. Jillian, clueless as to what they said, shot a look to Sabrina, who had been watching from behind her.

Sabrina nodded at her and stepped up beside her. The man turned back to them and eyed Sabrina. Jillian could swear that for a second a flicker of recognition registered in his eyes before his irritated expression returned.

"Again, like I said. I don't know your brother. Leave."

Jillian's heart sank. She'd been so hopeful that the man would be forthcoming and assure her that he'd seen her brother, that he'd been fine.

"Excuse me," Sabrina said.

The man looked over at the young woman.

"I know you," Sabrina said. "You went to Marcos de Niza high school."

"Si," the man replied. "That was a long time ago."

"It seems like ages ago," Sabrina answered. "We don't care about the car and don't want to call the police. All we want to do is find my friend's brother. Did he sell you his car?"

The man's posture softened and he opened the door wider. Not so much as to let them into his house but more so that the woman he'd spoken to seconds before could peer out and look at the two of them.

"As he said he bought the car fair and square," the woman replied.

"Of course he did. There is no question about that. But is my brother okay?"

The woman shrugged. The few seconds which followed seemed to be an eternity as the man weighed what he was going to say.

He looked over at Sabrina and locked in on Jillian. "I didn't see your brother. I met with a man who had the clean title to the car and it had been signed by the owner. I paid the man and got the car and title."

The woman disappeared for a minute and returned, nudging the man aside. "See."

She thrust a sheet of paper toward Jillian. Jillian reached for it, but the woman pulled it back. "No. You can look, but not take it."

"Okay, okay," Jillian replied.

The woman extended her arm. She scanned the document. Title, BMW, an almost unreadable spray of numbers and letters for the VIN and then she saw it. On the bottom. A signature. *Wesley Connors.*

"Is it his signature?" Sabrina asked.

"Yeah, I think it is. It looks like it," Jillian whispered.

"Gracias," Sabrina said.

The woman pulled back the car title. "You see, we bought the car."

"Yes. Thank you for your time," Sabrina replied.

Jillian felt Sabrina gently tug at her arm and pull her back from the door. "We're done."

"Where? Where did you meet the man and buy the car?" Jillian pleaded.

The couple remained silent.

"His name. Do you have the name of the man who sold you the car?"

Sabrina tightened her grip and began to pull Jillian back with more force.

"Please. His name."

"Martinez," the man replied brusquely, and then he closed the door.

Sabrina pulled Jillian down the walkway toward the street as the porch light switched off.

"Well I got a name," Jillian whispered.

The other woman didn't comment as she steered her to the sidewalk and down toward the car where Thomas was waiting. As they approached, he stepped out of the vehicle and asked, "How'd it go?"

"I got a name," Jillian replied.

The man glanced over at Sabrina. "Anyone we would recognize?"

The woman shook her head. "He said the man's name was Martinez. There's probably hundreds of people in the metro area with that last name. Might have as well given us the name Smith or Jones."

Jillian paused. *I never thought to ask for a full name. It might have been easier if I'd asked for the first name.* "I'm sorry. It never occurred to me to ask for a first name as well."

"We're not even sure that was the real name or if he just made something up," Sabrina answered quietly. "Don't beat yourself up too much. You did a great job, and we did learn some things."

"Such as?" Matt asked as he and Paul walked up.

"For starters, Wesley signed over the car title and sold the car," Sabrina replied.

Jillian tore her gaze away from the group and surveyed the area around them seeing two rows of houses with the lights out. "Where's Ian?"

Paul pointed behind her, and Jillian turned. Out of the shadows across the street, Ian emerged and he walked slowly toward the group. His handgun was in his left hand, and as he neared the group, he returned it to his holster.

"They looked terrified from my vantage point," he commented dryly.

"Yeah, I'd agree." Sabrina replied. "I believe from how they responded, they probably purchased the car in good faith. We know this much, that Wesley may have signed the title, but he actually didn't sell the car to them."

"Who did?" Ian asked.

"Someone named Martinez?" Thomas asked.

"Not much help," Paul added. "We're not going to successfully run that lead down."

"Agreed," Matt said. "Okay, we're done for tonight."

"Wait," Jillian responded. "That's it. That's all we're going to do?"

Ian walked over to her and laid his hand on her shoulder. The warmth of it sank into her shoulder chasing away the chill. "For right now, yes."

"We still have the tracking device on the car. We'll watch and see where these people go with it. Maybe it might open a reason to revisit them. But for the time being, there is no way if we call the police that we're going to get much more than we have now."

Jillian exhaled and rubbed her forehead. "Okay."

Ian dropped his grip from her shoulder and a cold heaviness descended upon her. She had hoped for much more than this meeting had produced.

"Okay everyone head home and get some sleep. Let's meet tomorrow at 9:30 for a recap back at the office," Matt said.

The group remained silent as they broke up and returned to their vehicles.

"Jillian, come on."

Weariness threaded through his voice. He appeared exhausted. With all the focus on what to say when she was walking to the house to speak with the guy who purchased her car, she hadn't noticed much of anything else, including the fact that Ian was across the street in the shadows with his gun drawn.

For a few seconds as they walked to his car she pondered what might have happened had the man who answered the door gotten combative, or worse pulled out a gun on her and Sabrina.

"Would you have fired your gun?" she asked.

Ian didn't immediately reply. Instead he clicked the remote, unlocking the car doors. He opened the passenger side door for her.

"You're not answering me. What would you have done if the man had pulled out a gun?"

"I'm not sure."

"Then why pull your gun?"

Ian closed the door, circled across the front of the car, and opened the driver's side door and slid in. He didn't speak as the inserted the keys and turned on the ignition. He sighed. "Habit. In Iraq you never knew whether the civilian you were talking to was a friend or foe. You were always on guard and prepared for a quick response if things went south."

If things went south. Jillian sank back into the seat of the car. Things had gone south for her brother. *Wesley, where are you?*

CHAPTER NINETEEN

Ian opened the door and turned on the switch. Light flooded the living room area, and Jillian stepped inside. She surveyed the room looking for Simon. She'd expected the cat at the door to greet them by the time they had entered the room, but he wasn't to be found.

"Simon?" Jillian said.

Ian tapped her on the shoulder and pointed to the Siamese cat who sauntered into the room and had paused to stretch and yawn. *Well, at least someone had managed to get a few hours of sleep.*

"Sorry we woke you up," Jillian murmured. The cat eyed her and didn't approach the couple, making his displeasure apparent.

"Hey, Buddy," Ian said quietly.

The cat looked at him and sat down and studied the couple. "Looks like he's a little miffed at us," Ian commented as he closed the door.

"If I had been awakened at three in the morning, I wouldn't be all that chipper either."

Jillian dropped her purse on the end table next to the sofa, raked her hand through her golden brown hair, and stretched. "I need a shower, and then I'm going to crash for a few hours. The good news is that I don't have to be at work during my regular time. I plan to squeeze in a few extra hours of sleep."

"Works for me," Ian replied. "You go first."

He gestured toward the hallway leading to the bathroom and bedroom. Jillian studied Ian. A five o-clock shadow graced his jaw and he moved as if was decades older that he actually was. He collapsed on the sofa, leaned back and closed his eyes. Maybe he'd been right when he'd suggested that Wesley had relapsed and started using drugs again. All the facts came together to indicate that.

"Ian, I think you've been right."

"What?"

She rubbed her face and her eyes watered in response. "You're right, Wesley has probably started using drugs again." She dropped her hands and looked at him, blurred through a wash of tears. "I've failed."

Ian stood up, walked over, and hugged her. She leaned into him while he stroked her hair and held her as she cried. He wrapped his arms around her and softly stroked her hair.

"Let it out," he whispered.

Jillian sucked in a ragged breath, then pulled back and looked at him. She'd half expected to see an 'I told you so' expression, but pain registered in his eyes.

"I'm sorry."

She tamped down the urge to continue to sob and wiped her eyes. "I have to update my parents and sister. What will they think?"

"Jilli, listen to me. Let them think what they want. You have to understand that you are not responsible for what has happened. You could not have stopped this. Drug addiction is a tough habit to kick permanently. Most people will, at one point or another, relapse."

She sniffed and nodded. "You're right. I know what you're saying is true, but it just doesn't feel that way. I feel as if I've failed. Wesley, my family, everyone."

Her throat tightened as another sob threatened to erupt.

Ian sighed and pulled her back to his chest. "I can't counsel you on how to emotionally let go. All I know is if you don't find some peace in your role, it will eat at you until..."

He tightened his embrace. Jillian exhaled and relaxed. The warmth of his body, the soft steady rise and fall of his chest with each breath, calmed her. She closed her eyes and wrapped her arms around him.

A few minutes later, Simon rubbed against her legs. His soft fur caressed one, then the other leg as he wrapped and wound himself around them. Jillian open her eyes and gazed at the cat.

"Looks like at least Simon has forgiven you," Ian said. "See, it's an omen of things to come."

Jillian snorted a soft laugh. "Yeah right. My cat never really clicked with Wes. I suspect my parents will take longer to come around."

"Well, if they won't listen to you, I'll have a few words with them and set them straight."

"That would be a surprise," Jillian said as she looked at Ian. "With all that has happened, I've forgotten to let them know that you're back."

Ian let her go. "What are you going to say?"

Jillian bit her lip. "The truth. I hired Sonoran Security to help find Wes and you were assigned to the case. Truth be known, I'm not sure if they'll be happy about that either."

Ian's dark brown eyes narrowed. "Oh?"

Jillian took in a slow, deep breath and exhaled. "When you enlisted and left, it hurt. A lot. They love me and worried that you'd hurt me again."

"You hurt me. You went off to college and left me behind as if all we had didn't matter. Granted it was high school, but I believe what we had was special. The real thing. Then once you left, they told me you were seeing someone else. What was I supposed to do? Wait? Say nothing? Put up with it?"

She closed her eyes. *Here it comes. The issue that has been lurking in the shadows since we started searching for Wesley.* Jillian took a couple steps back and trained her gaze on Ian's face. Strange, behind the anger and suspicion in his eyes, there was something she hadn't caught years ago, fear and pain.

"Ian, please listen to me. I don't want to get into a fight about this. Not now with so much at stake, but everyone expected me to go on to college. Heck, I wanted it. A chance to stretch myself, to learn and grow. *To be sure about us.* I never stepped out on you. There was never anyone else."

Jillian studied him. The cocktail of emotions she had witnessed seconds before appeared to have faded a bit. She'd stopped short of saying there hadn't been anyone else then or since.

Stepping forward, Jillian placed her hand on his arm. "Hey."

He blinked, looked away, and pulled back a few steps. "You're right. We can't fight right now about this. We need to let it go."

Jillian wrapped her arms around herself. "Okay. I agree. But at some point we need to have a talk so we can move on."

He looked back. "You hurt me too," Ian whispered. "It hurt so much I ran away. To the other side of the planet, to war and death." He shook his head. "I'm so tired. Of the pain, of all of it."

"So am I," Jillian said.

Ian nodded. "Go get a shower."

Conversation is over. Jillian turned, walked over, and picked up her purse. Instinctively, she checked her phone for messages.

She swiped the screen and clicked on the text messages. A few odd Facebook posts peppered the list. A text from Larry stood out. *We need to talk ASAP. Call me.*

Jillian noted the time. Should she call? It was close to four in the morning and after all that had happened, she didn't have adrenaline at this point. Images of her car with the bullet hole in the windshield and the slashed tires flickered in her mind. Had Rossi made good on his threats?

"What?" Ian asked.

She held up the screen, as if she thought he could read the text from the few feet away. "Larry texted me and said to call."

"Has he followed up the text with any others or has he called?"

Jillian scrolled through the list of text. "No." She tapped in a reply, *What's up?*

"It's so late, I don't expect I'll hear…"

The phone pinged. Larry's response was short and direct. *Get over here now. Don't call the police. I'm in the storage room.*

CHAPTER TWENTY

Jillian hadn't spoken a word since they'd left his apartment, but she didn't need to. She'd immediately called Larry and he did not reply. It didn't take a psychic to know that she anticipated some additional vandalism. The question that neither of them were willing to ask out loud was simple: how bad was it?

At this point, he was ready to bet the farm on what had been his working theory. Wesley had relapsed and began using drugs again. Everything they'd discovered so far fit perfectly into his assessment. Now, even Jillian had finally given up the hope that something else had happened.

Had Rossi made good on his threat? Lord only knows what a man might do for fifty thousand dollars, but given the man's background, it could be bad. The head chef's text had been cryptic.

Shawn was on the way in to join them at La Villa de Gardenia. When he'd called his brother, Ian updated him on the activities at the pawn shop and Jillian's conversation with the man that Wesley had apparently sold his car to. Shawn made no comment. He knew his brother well enough to know that he was sorting through the facts and evaluating the options.

He glanced over to Jillian. She had gone still as she leaned forward and peered out the front window as they pulled into the parking lot. Ian quickly scanned the car lot and found only one car parked by the employee's entrance in the east side of the building.

"The building looks okay," Jillian said softly.

"Yep," Ian replied. "Is that Larry's car?"

"Yes," Jillian said.

Ian pulled up beside the dark green Jeep and turned off the engine. "I would prefer to wait until Shawn arrives before we go in."

He shouldn't have bothered speaking, as Jillian opened the door, clutched her purse, and walked briskly to the back entrance.

Ian hissed a curse, flipped off the car lights, and raced to join her. "Jillian, wait."

As she jammed the key into the door lock with a fumbling hand, Ian cupped his hand over hers. "Stop, Jilli. Stop."

Jillian looked over her shoulder at him. Concern, bordering on near panic, played in her eyes. "What if it's Wesley? What if he's found Wesley?"

The soft noise of an engine purred into the night. Ian let go of Jillian's hand as Shawn's black SUV pulled into the parking lot. *Thank God, Shawn's here.*

"It's Shawn," Ian said. "Just give us a minute. Please."

"Fine." Jillian removed the key from the lock.

"Hell of a night," Shawn mused aloud as he walked up to them.

"You could say that," Ian replied.

Shawn cocked his head to the side as he eyed Jillian. "Did Larry disclose the reason why you needed to be here so quickly?"

Jillian shook her head. "No. I tried calling him on his cell, but he didn't pick up. He's been waiting for hours. When I responded to his text, his reply was almost immediate. It can't be good." She laced her hands through her hair, pulling the tangled strands from her face. "What if he's found Wesley?"

"If he had, there would have been no reason to hold that information back from you," Shawn answered. "Okay. Give me the details. When we enter this door, what room are we walking into and what is the route to the storage room?"

At his calm, unemotional tone, the fear in Jillian's eyes eased. The adrenaline buzz in Ian also ratcheted down a notch as well.

"We're going into the kitchen. The walk-in freezer and refrigerator are off to the left. We set up this entrance for ease of taking deliveries. Once we walk through the kitchen, we step outside into the courtyard, but we'll be under the covered walkway. From there, we'll turn right and head down about three hundred feet and to a door on our right. That's where we store our tables, chairs, dishes, linens, you name it."

"Did Larry say where to meet him?" Shawn asked.

"No. Just that he was in the storage room," Jillian replied.

"Are there any other entrances or exits to the storage room than the one we're going to?" Ian asked.

"No."

"Any alarms?"

"No."

"Okay." Shawn said. "You two lead the way. I'm counting to twenty then I'm following. Hopefully you won't need reinforcements. Got it?"

"Yep," Ian replied.

Jillian unlocked the door. The kitchen lights were on and the three of them stepped in. Ian scanned the area. Stainless steel counters gleamed beneath the kitchens' fluorescent lights. Pots, pans, and other cooking utensils stood in organized stacks. Ian even cast a glance at the recycle bin where he'd tossed the water bottle into a while back. Even that was empty.

He glanced at his brother and then asked, "Jillian, is there anything out of place here?"

"No," she answered hoarsely. She locked eyes with him and the concern in her eyes was rapidly building into panic. "Follow me." Jillian strode across the kitchen.

From the doorway leading to the covered open hallway, Jillian glanced back at him and then opened door and left the kitchen without comment. She actually held the door for him as he walked through and pointed down the covered hallway, which skirted the perimeter of the courtyard.

He didn't like it. The lights were off. The arches that decorated the corridor, while attractive in the light of day, only served to obstruct what little light the moon gave off. Jillian fished out her cell phone, tapped on it and turned on some sort of a flashlight app. It wasn't exactly a true flashlight, but it did provide some illumination.

Ian liked this even less. If someone wanted to take a shot at them, it wouldn't be hard to miss.

Jillian picked up the pace slightly as she led the way to the storage room.

In the distance, Ian thought he saw a pin-sized light. It moved upward, brightened, and then dropped several feet. The smell of tobacco smoke drifted in the air, and from the shadows he heard the head chef's voice. "What took you so long?"

Jillian strode quickly toward Larry. "What's going on?"

"You tell me," Larry replied in a voice mixed with thinly veiled anger and distrust. Jillian cast a puzzled look at Ian.

"Hey," Ian snapped back. "Take it easy and just tell us why all the drama at this hour."

Larry took another pull from his cigarette and then stepped over and extinguished it in the ashtray section of one of those combo trashcan/ashtray containers.

"Come with me," the chef said gruffly.

He walked into the storage area and flipped on the light switch. The space flooded with light and Ian surveyed the area.

"Teardown went smoothly last night," Larry said. "The wedding reception ended close to nine-thirty. About an hour after you two left."

The chef walked past a couple rows containing chairs and tables.

"The team had placed the dishes and glassware back and I was doing a quick walk-through when I noticed something. A box which wasn't here a couple days ago."

Jillian and Ian followed the chef as he took a right turn and headed to the back of an aisle with shelves of neatly stacked glasses and dishes. The chef stopped abruptly and pointed to a corrugated box tucked in the corner of a bottom shelf. "That."

Jillian exhaled and looked at Ian with a mix of exhaustion and puzzlement. Clearly, she had no clue what the chef was upset about.

"Let me," Ian replied as he walked to the shelf and bent over to open the box.

The chef stepped back a few steps as Ian approached. It didn't take a brain surgeon to note the man appeared to be bracing for a fight. Ian paused to look at him for a couple of seconds. The man pointed to the box and said nothing. Ian squatted, opened the corrugated panels, and looked inside. For a few seconds he stared as it took a few seconds to identify what he saw. He hissed a curse.

"What is it?" Jillian asked.

"Drugs," Shawn replied.

The three turned and caught Shawn standing at the end of the aisle.

"Who the hell are you?" Larry asked. The suspicion in the man's voice was rapidly giving way to panic.

"Relax. It's okay," Ian said.

Shawn walked slowly to the group. "I'm Shawn Randall, and I co-own Sonoran Security. We've been retained by Ms. Connors to locate her missing brother."

Larry cast a surprised look at Jillian. "Wes is missing? Since when?"

Ian remembered when this had started, Jillian had gone out of her way to not let the employees know what had happened. Now that the news was out, it would be a matter of a few hours before everyone knew.

Jillian's face had gone almost ashen as she returned her gaze from the chef to the small-sized box that Ian continued to kneel by. "A couple of days ago."

Shawn walked up to Ian, who without a word pulled back the flaps to the box so his brother could see inside. A cache of small plastic packets of white powder were stacked in the box.

"Cocaine?" Shawn asked.

"Maybe," Ian replied. "It looks less like powder from what I can see. More like granulated sugar. Could be meth."

"Oh, dear God." Jillian exhaled as she reached up and rubbed the center of her forehead.

"Who has access to this room?" Shawn asked.

"Larry and I have a key to the area. But in the last couple of days tons of people actually had access. We had to pull supplies in and out before and after the wedding."

"Yeah, she's right," Larry said.

"Jillian," Ian said as he stood up from the box. "You need to call the police. Now."

"Yes," she replied in a soft, dull voice while nodding. She glanced over at Larry. "Thank you."

The chef shrugged. "Felt you should know first." He then frowned at Ian and Shawn. "Do you have any idea what happened to her brother?"

"We're working on that," Shawn replied.

Chapter Twenty-One

Jillian walked into the apartment, dropped her purse and sank onto the sofa. She stared up at the ceiling. Ian closed the door and turned the deadbolt on the door with a snap. He disappeared into the kitchen.

The tinkle of ice dropping into a glass was followed by the soft thump of a freezer door closing. Moments later, he rounded the door, extending a glass with amber-colored liquid in it. "Here."

Without comment, she grasped the glass and gently swirled the drink. Jillian took a sip and winced. "What is this?"

"Whiskey."

"Tastes like paint thinner."

Ian chuckled, raised his hand, and issued a small salute of sorts. "Bottoms up."

Jillian took another sip, and then set the glass down on the coffee table as she absently scratched Simon behind the ears when he brushed up against her ankle. "Well, if I thought before today that things could not possibly get worse, I was wrong. They have."

Ian sat down in the large overstuffed chair near her. "Yeah. Even though you called the police, the fact is the drugs were found in your storage room, which makes you a person of interest."

"I haven't spoken to my parents or sister in over twenty-four hours. I need to update them. About everything."

She looked up and met Ian's coffee-colored eyes. She could get lost in their depths.

"Speaking of parents, I haven't seen your parents in almost a decade. How are they doing?" Jillian asked quietly.

"Fine. Still hold their season tickets to the Cardinals. Have gotten to be quite the tailgate partiers. Dad takes pride in turning out a first rate barbecue before each game."

"Sounds like you know that from first-hand experience," Jillian replied.

Ian crooked a small grin. "Yep." He took another sip from his drink. "They threw a party when I came home and I joined them at several of the football games."

Jillian picked up her whiskey from the end table. "And you're back safe and sound."

Ian softly shook his head. "I'm here, but I've not really returned home. Yet."

He gazed at the half-empty glass in his hand and appeared to be considering something. Slowly he leaned forward and placed the drink on the coffee table.

"What was it like?"

Ian didn't answer.

"Ian, talk to me. You had some horrific dream the other night. When you awoke, you were darn near in a full panic. What happened?"

The relaxed, tired expression faded from his features, and he tightly closed his eyes as if in pain. "It was bad. The death and the destruction."

He opened his eyes, which revealed a deep pain within their depths. "I saw one of my best buddies get run over by a car. The SOB meant to hit him. Raul didn't have time to get out of the way."

"That was the nightmare the other night," Jillian stated.

Ian nodded. "We thought we were liberating them from a dictator. Making the world a safer place. But for many, we weren't the good guys. Instead, the U.S. Military was just another occupying force to wage guerrilla warfare. If they couldn't make us leave, then they'd make us wish we had."

Jillian rose from the chair, knelt next to him, and gently rubbed his hand. It was a silly gesture, some feeble effort at comforting a hurting friend, but she dared not do more for fear of where it could lead. They'd kissed a couple times in the past couple days and instinctively she knew that with little effort they could end up in bed. After all these years apart, she wasn't ready for that. Not yet, not until this whole mess was settled. If he left her life when this case was over, then she'd have to live with that. Find closure. Move on.

He drilled his thumb into his brow and sank back into the chair. The tension eased from his face. She gently released his hand, stood up and gently kissed him on the temple. Then she walked to the bedroom and prepared to take a shower.

Jillian needed to crank the temperature up, let the hot water loosen all the tense muscles in her back and neck, and then hopefully she'd get a few hours of sleep.

The police had taken the drugs. They'd informed her that the lab would provide the identification as to what was exactly in the small plastic packages, but based upon what it looked like, their initial assessment matched what Ian had guessed. Meth.

She opened the closet, pulled out an oversized cotton tunic, and pulled on pants in a soft shade of gray along with her terry robe. So much for sexy, alluring apparel. This outfit was as far on the other end of the scale as she could have gotten.

She gathered the items in her arms and marched to the bathroom. As she flipped on the light and closed the door, she glanced in the mirror. Dark circles had developed under her eyes, and the makeup, applied long ago, had faded to the point that it looked like she hadn't applied any.

While the police had interrogated her and Larry, it had been clear they were under suspicion. Jillian believed the only thing that may have prevented them both being hauled downtown for further questioning was that a number of people could have had access to the storage area.

Jillian raked her hand through her hair and pushed it away from her face. She wondered who would have placed them there. Larry had been with her for a couple of years, and the head chef appeared to be an honest, hard-working guy who would never get involved with trafficking Nothing in his lifestyle indicated he was raking in major money on the side, from the clothes he wore, to his house, and twenty-five year plus marriage to his wife. Nothing matched with the image of a drug dealer.

Turning on the faucet, she grabbed the toothbrush and toothpaste that rested vertically in a glass in the corner of the counter. Someone else who worked for her had to be the guilty party. *The question was, who?*

Jillian began to brush her teeth. She supposed they would know soon. There had to be fingerprints or something on the box, or in it, which would give the police a clue. Hopefully, they'd determine who was responsible and arrest them.

She spat into the sink. Drugs. What in the world was going on? It just seemed this problem was touching her in many ways.

She didn't smoke, rarely drank alcohol, and for darn sure never did drugs. Apparently, she was some naïve Pollyanna.

Jillian considered. Until her life had been upended, her normal routine meant she watched the ten p.m. news every night. Most cases there was one or more shootings, convenience store robberies, and even some car chase. Now the dots were starting to connect. Drugs were touching many more lives than just hers.

She placed the toothbrush back in the glass jar and turned on the shower. Ian had been correct. Wesley had relapsed and somewhere out there he was probably staying in some crappy rat hole, either high or crashing. The question was where? The bigger question, would they find him in time?

***

Ian sucked in a deep breath and opened his eyes. He scanned the room and the dream faded as thoughts of the here and now pushed into his conscious mind.

He'd been there again, in his dreams. This time it was a bit different. Instead of being in the middle of it and re-living everything, he'd floated above it all, like he was some kind of drone.

Gracing the tops of buildings, he looked into courtyards and saw people going about their daily tasks. They ignored him or behaved as if they didn't know he was there. Men with beards wore loose robes, or some thrown together version of western apparel, and moved among women in figureless abayas while preschool children played.

He hadn't awoke in a full-on panic as he usually did when he dreamed of being in Iraq. For the first time, there was some kind of emotional distancing that he'd never experienced before.

"Thank you, God," he whispered as he lightly scratched his chest.

Could it have been because he'd talked to Jillian about what had happened in Iraq? Ian had spent so much of his energy trying not to talk about his experience, even resisting Shawn's suggestion that maybe he needed to get some counseling. Maybe his brother was right. He wasn't sure if it was more a case of getting the past off his chest or whether Jillian's compassionate reaction registered at some level as acceptance, he wasn't sure. But for the first time in a while he actually felt a bit lighter, calmer. Maybe he needed therapy, or at least someone to talk to who could help him sort things out.

Ian glanced down at this watch to check the time. Yeah, he needed a few more hours and then would drop her off at work and head into the office. He needed to see if there were any additional updates.

Speaking of, Jillian was going to make some phone calls later to update her parents and sister about all that had transpired within the last twenty-four hours. From what she had said, it was clear Jillian believed that they expected her to be the person who kept her brother clean and sober.

Irritation buzzed softly through him. If they gave her grief about that, he wasn't sure he would be able to sit by calmly and let them rain down their fear and frustration on her. Jillian said they weren't aware that he was back or working on the case to find Wesley. Well, if he jumped into the conversation, wouldn't they be surprised.

CHAPTER TWENTY-TWO

Coffee. Ian smelled coffee. He opened his eyes and caught the light on in the kitchen. Simon meowed.

"Here you go. Bon appétit," Jillian said.

Apparently, she was feeding the cat. Ian checked his watch. Twelve thirty-seven.

Jillian exited the galley kitchen and set a mug on the table. She glanced over at him and smiled. "You're awake. I tried to be as quiet as I could, but Simon was hungry and he was driving me nuts."

"No problem, it was time I got up anyway." He rubbed his face and felt the stubble of a day's growth of beard on his chin.

"Would you like some?" Jillian raised her mug up to him.

"Yeah, give me a minute." Ian sat up, then made a quick trip to the bathroom and returned to find that she had a cup waiting for him with the sugar bowl and spoon set next to the brew.

He sat down at the small dining room table next to the kitchen, added some sugar, and took a sip.

"I was thinking," Jillian said.

Ian studied her and tried to read her facial expression. "Yeah."

"Rossi." She set her mug down and picked up Simon, who had been hovering around her feet. Jillian cradled the cat to her and gently scratched under his chin. The Siamese rolled his head back and purred loudly. "It doesn't make sense. The guy calls, searching for Wes, says Wes owes him fifty thousand dollars, and if I can't find my brother, he expects me to make good on paying the debt. Rossi has information on me. Stuff that he shouldn't have, not unless Wesley provided it to him."

Jillian stopped petting the cat for a moment to take another sip of coffee. "My brother, in addition to stealing my stuff, has committed identity theft. I mean, Rossi said he had my signature on the papers." Jillian glanced over at Ian. "I never signed anything."

"Yep."

"Strange, wouldn't you think that if someone thought you owed them fifty thousand dollars, and you'd gone as far as to vandalize their car to make a point, would you stop pursuing them for the money? Think about it. I haven't heard from this scumbag for a couple days. That doesn't make sense."

Ian took another sip from his mug. *She's right. The phone calls have stopped. Why?*

Ian watched Jillian as she stared out the window and continued to pet her cat. She was lost in thought. Was she thinking what he was? That Rossi may have found Wesley first and they were too late?

"I know you didn't approve of me not telling the police about Rossi yesterday. But it was obvious they suspected that either Larry, me, or one of my employees is trafficking the stuff. It looked bad enough that only Larry and I have a set of keys to the storage room. Probably the only reason they didn't haul both of us downtown was because with tearing down the furniture for yesterday's wedding, it really could have been anyone. A lot of people had access to the storage area last night."

She set the cat down softly on the floor. "I'm calling my family this afternoon with an update. They're going to conclude what you and I have. Wesley is using again."

Jillian locked a stare at Ian. "They are going to be stunned about Rossi and that their son's probably blown his inheritance. But how do I explain the fact that Rossi hasn't contacted me for two days?"

Ian didn't reply. Jillian didn't seem to want an answer. She was sorting things out and coming to a possible conclusion as to what may have happened to her brother.

"What are you going to do?" Ian asked.

"I'm going to press charges against Wes for theft."

Ian arched an eyebrow. "Okay."

"With some of the stuff in the ninety-day hold at the pawn shop and their documentation, there's no doubt he sold it."

Jillian's voice took on a cool, determined tone. "Wes must deal with the consequences of his choices. I can't shelter him from that. My family can't either."

Calm resignation graced her face. "I have one more thing I must do," Jillian stated softly.

"Oh?"

"Contact Rossi. I need to see if I can get some closure on that front. If he wants the money, I'll pay it and get him the hell out of my life. Maybe Wesley's too."

"Why?" Ian asked. "If he's stopped contacting you, maybe he's decided to walk away."

"I doubt that. I can't keep looking over my shoulder wondering when he'll surface again. Besides, if I pay, he'll leave Wes alone."

Ian didn't comment. What more could he add? Jillian had clearly arrived at a tipping point on what needed to be done, and for what it was worth, he was on board with her choices.

"What's today's schedule?"

Jillian took a sip of her coffee. "Not much. Frankly, despite a few hours of sleep, I'm still tired. Going to check on the status of my car. Maybe get an ETA as to when it will be ready for pick up." She smiled. "You've been great, but you cannot continue to chauffeur me around."

Ian smiled. "I don't mind."

Jillian rose, went to her purse, and pulled out her phone. She turned it on and scrolled through a screen.

"What are you looking for?" Ian asked.

"Rossi. Time to call him." She glanced over at him and her expression hardened to one of determination. "This is my last gift to my brother. I'm going to pay for his freedom, and mine, from this man."

"It's a lot of money. Maybe you should wait a day or so."

"I would wait. But Wesley can't. He's out there somewhere and if they find him first, God only knows what may happen."

She punched the button to dial and switched to speaker phone mode so Ian could hear. The phone rang several times and went to voice mail. Strange, Ian thought. There was no recorded introduction asking the caller to leave a message. Just an abrupt beep.

"This is Jillian Connors. I'm leaving a message to let you know I have the funds you requested. Call me back."

She disconnected the call by punching the bottom in one quick stroke. "Now we wait."

Ian got up and checked his phone messages. "Got a text from Matt. He's calling a meeting at the office in a little less than two hours to recap everything."

"Do I need to be there?" Jillian asked.

"Probably not. I can drop you off at work if you need to go there."

"Thanks."

"If you need to use the bathroom to get ready for work, you go first," Ian said.

Jillian stood up, tucked the chair underneath the table, and headed through the living room and down the hall. "I won't take too long."

Ian stared out the window and finished his coffee. He needed every bit of the caffeine in it to make it through to this evening. Perhaps it was more emotional burnout from the rollercoaster of the past twenty-four hours of discoveries.

The sad part was they were no closer to finding Wesley than they were when this case started. All Sonoran Security had been able to do was follow Wesley's trail.

Ian didn't envy her the task ahead. When her family was updated, how would they handle it? Were they aware that while he'd stayed with his sister, Wesley hadn't been terribly cooperative? He'd rebelled and chose not to keep Jillian updated about what was going on. Classic behavior for someone who was hiding something.

Jillian's phone pinged and she returned from the bedroom a couple minutes later. She'd now sported a pair of dress slacks and matching top. Tucked over the crook in her elbow hung a jacket. The deep olive green of the outfit brought out soft red highlights in her hair. She set the jacket down. "The bathroom is all yours," she announced.

"Thanks. I think you got a text or an email."

Jillian picked up the phone. "Okay."

She swiped the screen and poked down. Ian stood up and began to walk back to the bathroom. "Ian. Take a look at this."

He walked back. Jillian held out the phone for him to read the message.

Bro has manned up and made good. You're off the hook.

She chewed on her lower lip.

"Rossi?"

She nodded. What had Wesley done that could have made Rossi drop his pursuit of Jillian for his fifty thousand dollars? Give the guy the monies from the sale of his car and the money from the pawn shop sales? Apparently, but with all that, Ian figured he still was far short of the amount that Rossi claimed Jillian's brother owed him. What did Rossi mean by saying Wesley had manned up?

CHAPTER TWENTY-THREE

Ian entered the conference room. "Sorry, I'm late. Had to drop Jillian off to pick up her car from the dealership."

No one responded and he quickly assessed the team. The silence from everyone could be summed up with one word: exhaustion.

"Let's gets through this as quickly as we can," Matt announced.

Ian took a chair. "I've got some updates."

All heads turned in his direction. "What?" Shawn asked.

"Jillian and I were talking earlier. She has finally concluded that her brother has relapsed and is using drugs again."

"About time," Thomas commented softly.

Matt tossed a disapproving glance at the young man and then returned his focus to Ian. "That's it?"

"Nope. She zeroed in on the fact that we'd not heard from Rossi. Let's face it, he calls her, states that she co-signed a loan for fifty thousand for her brother. She denies this and suddenly her car gets mysteriously vandalized. Interesting coincidence. She's received follow up calls from him and then suddenly they stop. No explanation, no further contact. Why?"

"So?" Paul asked.

"Earlier today, she called him and left a voice message and we got an answer. Rossi's text basically said Wesley had 'manned up' and that she was off the hook."

"Oh God," Shawn muttered.

"That could mean any number of things," Sabrina added.

"Yeah." Ian said. "The way I do the math, even with the monies from the stuff he took from Jillian's and the sale of his car, he's short several thousand dollars. And that begs the question: what else had been stolen and sold to pay for this?"

"It could also mean that Wesley is dead," Thomas added.

The room went silent for almost a minute. Thomas' assessment was the acknowledgement of the eight hundred-pound gorilla in the room. Everyone just looked at each other expecting someone to speak first.

Sabrina sighed. "Rossi didn't say that Wesley was dead. Right?"

"Not explicitly," Ian replied. "For what it's worth, he didn't even leave his name."

"If I were Rossi, I would never so much as much hint that was what happened," Thomas said quietly.

"No," Sabrina replied. "Killing doesn't make sense. If Jillian's brother had actually come up with a sizable part of the monies owed, then it would be in Rossi's best interest to let Wesley Connors continue to come up with the rest of the money."

Ian glanced over at Shawn. His brother played quietly with the pen in his hand. After a few moments, Shawn spoke. "Sabrina's right. If Wesley came up with part of it within three days, then he may have bought some time to come up with the rest."

His brother looked at Ian and his lips curled into a soft hint of grin. "Jillian may be off the hook, but Wesley isn't. That leaves us with where we were three days ago. Where is Wesley Connors?"

Matt leaned back and exhaled. Shawn shook his head. "Ian, you might let Jillian know we're at a point where we have little that we can follow up on to find her brother."

"I know," Ian replied. "For what it's worth, I believe that even Jillian knows that. She's making a phone call this afternoon to update her family as to what has happened within the last twenty-four hours." Ian shook his head. "Her parents are holding out hope that Wesley will turn up, sober and with some reasonable explanation as to what went on. Jillian thinks her family is going to hold her responsible for his relapse."

Paul whispered a curse and Sabrina muttered, "They are idiots."

The group stared at Sabrina, surprised the quiet woman had spoken so bluntly.

"What?" she protested as she matched their shocked stares.

"Okay," Shawn said. "Next steps. What are the police doing since she has reported the finding of the drugs in her storage room?"

"No update," Matt answered. "Probably they've identified exactly what the substance was, are putting the puzzle pieces together, and seeing what fits."

"Should we consider adding security cameras or something like that?" Thomas asked.

"Nope," Shawn answered. "We're not mixing into this. Let the police do their job. Let Jillian know we're at a dead end for the time being."

"Done."

"Okay, meeting over," Matt said.

***

Jillian took a couple of large swallows from her diet soda, glanced at her watch, and pondered where her brother could be.

"Penny for your thoughts."

Ian stood at her office door and she smiled. "Hey."

He entered the room and closed the door with a soft click behind him. "How'd it go with your talk?"

"Better than I expected. It appears that the past couple of days have given everyone time to process things, and my family has come to the same conclusion. I was so worried that they were going to hold me responsible for Wesley, but they didn't," Jillian said.

Ian sank into the chair in front of her desk. "Good."

She drank in the image of him as he settled into the chair. So much about him had changed over the years. Gone was man who liked to tease and flirt with her, but at times there were fleeting moments, when she spied the old Ian. Jillian studied his dark hair with the subtle copper undertones and his coffee-colored eyes. He'd left to see the world and in his gaze she saw that the experience had shaped him into a more reserved, less trusting man.

Ian looked over at her and arched an eyebrow. *Did she take a chance?*

"What?" he said quietly before a soft smile broke on his lips.

Oh, just go for it, the voice in her head chided. Jillian slowly stood up. She had worked to push him back after the first day, she wondered what he would do if she opened that door again. She was scared that if she got emotionally involved again when this was over he'd walk away. "Can you do me a favor? I could really use a hug right now."

The seconds that followed seemed like an eternity. Ian arose from the chair, and opened his arms. "Come here."

She skirted around the desk and into his arms. He drew her in. No polite, soft shoulder hug where you leaned in but didn't really get close. Full body contact. Jillian laid her head on his chest and whispered, "The past two days have been crazy."

Ian didn't reply but simply held her. Jillian looked at him and wiggled out of his arms. "Ian?"

He drew her back to him. "I'm sorry, Jilli, we're at a dead end right now with trying to find Wesley."

"I know."

He pulled back. "Are you okay?"

"No," Jillian replied. "But there isn't anything that I can do about it. Except hope and pray Wesley turns up, and I need to pick up my things and Simon. It's time I move back into my place."

Pain quickly appeared and then faded from Ian's eyes. "Okay, but let me take you to dinner. Not some fast food dash, but a nice, proper, sit-down dinner."

Her stomach fluttered as she realized he didn't want to walk away. "That would be nice. But nothing too fancy."

"Got it. Italian?"

CHAPTER TWENTY-FOUR

Jillian bolted straight up in bed. The phone rang a second time and she glanced over at the cell on her nightstand and the number on it. She swiped the screen and answered. "Hello?"

"Ms. Connors?" The voice was calm, low, and masculine.

"Yes?"

"This is Detective Alward. We have apprehended two men who've broken into your storage room."

Jillian swept her hair back away from the side of her face. *They've caught the guys who placed the drugs in my storage room.* "Uh, okay," she stammered. "You're still at La Villa?"

"Yes, we would like you to come down and see if you know who these men are."

"I'm on my way," Jillian replied.

After disconnecting the call, she slid out of bed and hurried over to her closet, slid into a pair of jeans and a pull-over sweater, and scurried to the bathroom where she brushed her hair.

Within minutes, Jillian slid into car, turned on the ignition and opened the garage door. In the darkness, she glanced over at the clock on the dashboard. *Two forty-three.* She bit her lip. Should she call Ian? Lord knows he could probably use an uninterrupted night's sleep, but he'd probably be angry if she didn't keep him in the loop about this development.

Jillian decided sleepless was better than angry and grabbed her phone.

"Yeah," Ian said.

He sounded groggy, tired, and a trace of irritation crackled through his voice.

"Ian. I just got a call from the police. They caught a couple of men who got into my storage room. I'm on my way over to La Villa."

If Ian hadn't been awake when he answered, he was now. "I'll meet you there."

"Thanks."

He disconnected, and Jillian tossed the phone onto the passenger's seat. At least it appeared that something was being resolved. Thank goodness, she was finally getting a break on at least something.

Twenty minutes later, she pulled into the parking lot. Blue and red flashing lights signaled where the squad cars were situated. As she crossed the expanse of black asphalt toward them Jillian could see shadowed figures moving between the patrol cars and a few officers exiting from the back entrance to her building. She pulled up and parked several spaces away from the collection of police vehicles. She slowly emerged from her BMW.

A uniformed policeman watched her approach. "I'm Jillian Connors. Detective Alward called about a break-in."

The officer nodded. "Wait here. Stay away from the two police cars over there. Do not approach or talk to the men inside."

"No problem," Jillian replied. The officer stepped away, but as she waited for the detective to return, she couldn't stop herself from staring at the two vehicles. *They're inside those cars.* She stared at the darkened windows in the back seat, hoping to catch a glimpse of who might be inside. Would she recognize them? Did she know who they were?

The lights of another car pulling up flooded the area. Ian's car pulled up and parked next to hers. The nervous edge which had caused her torso to tighten into a hard knot uncoiled slightly. Ian stepped out of his car and walked slowly up to her. His hair was as tousled as the white t-shirt which looked as if he'd slept in it. Five o'clock shadow had become a 'five a.m. shadow' and only seemed to call attention to the wary look in his eyes.

"Well?" Ian asked.

"I've been told to wait here. I'm guessing the detective will come out shortly.

"Where are they?"

"Over there. I think." Jillian pointed to the two squad cars.

Ian took a few steps toward the vehicles and Jillian grasped his arm. "No, don't."

He glanced at her with a puzzled expression.

"The officer told me to stay here and specifically not to approach them."

Ian shrugged. "Okay."

They stood in silence and waited. A soft cool breeze rustled through the trees on the property. Jillian studied Ian as he surveyed the property. He turned to glance back at her and his eyes were threaded with concern.

"What?" Jillian asked softly.

"I've got a bad feeling about this." Ian paused. "I would have thought that the detective would have come out sooner. It's been several minutes. Something isn't right."

Ian had a point. They had been standing and waiting here for close to ten minutes. If it had been important enough to have come out immediately, it would have made sense that the detective would have talked to her by now.

She glanced over at the back entrance the officer had gone into. "You don't suppose these guys did some damage inside?"

"Maybe," Ian said. "Maybe they found more drugs."

"This has been one long, never-ending nightmare," Jillian whispered.

"Yes it has," Ian growled back.

Clearly, the long hours and the chasing of dead end leads were wearing on Ian too. Jillian glanced over at him as he scanned the surroundings and she sensed the tension which rolled off him.

"Ian?"

He turned and looked at her. Words eluded her. What could she say after an awkward silence? "I'm so sorry. I shouldn't have come to Sonoran Security and dragged you into all of this. Some other agency might have been able to deal with all…"

"Don't," Ian replied. "Don't apologize. If anything, we've failed you. We're three days into this case, and we've little to show for it. Your brother is still missing and now this." Ian gestured at the cars several yards away and then raked his hand through his hair. "I've failed you. Not the other way around. "

"Ian, no," Jillian whispered. "Look at me."

He locked his eyes on her.

"No. It's not your fault." She stepped forward, and swept the errant hair back from his brow. "The last few days, I've had to come to terms with the fact that there is only so much that I can do. Wesley is responsible for whatever mess he's gotten himself into. I can't save the world and I certainly can't stop him from the path he's taken."

She paused and watched his face. "We do the best we can. But sometimes our best isn't enough." Jillian gently traced her hand down the side of his face. Ian opened his mouth as if to argue and she gently laid her fingers to his lips to silence him.

"I see it in your eyes. The memories, the guilt. It fuels your nightmares and haunts you every day. If you don't find a way to let it go, in time it will destroy you."

Ian whispered. "How do I forget?"

"It's not about forgetting. It's about forgiving. Yourself."

He took in what she said in silence.

"Ms. Connors."

Jillian dropped her hand and stepped away from Ian. An older man in dress slacks walked toward her, followed by the officer that she'd spoken to earlier.

The man's blue eyes held a suspicious 'all business' vibe. He pulled out and handed her a business card. "Detective John Alward."

He trained his focus on Ian. "You are?"

"Ian Randall. Ms. Connors has hired our agency to assist in finding her missing brother."

The detective nodded. "Any success in locating him?"

Ian glanced over at Jillian as if he was considering how much to reveal to the police. "We've pursued some leads. So far, they've been dead ends."

The man returned his gaze to Jillian. "Yesterday, you called because you discovered a suspicious parcel in your storage area. You suspected that it could have been drugs. I can confirm that after preliminary tests, the substance was crystal meth. We've waited and watched. Whoever placed the drugs in your storage room would eventually return to retrieve them. We didn't have to wait long. We have two men in custody who late last night broke into your storage room."

"So how did they break in?"

"They didn't break in," Alward replied dryly.

Jillian returned her attention back to the older man only to find him studying her closely. "I'm sorry. I don't understand. How did they get into my company's storage room?"

"With a key," the detective replied.

Jillian's mouth gaped and she glanced over at the two darkened police cruisers. "A key? But the only two people who have a key are Larry and..." Jillian stopped and glanced over at Ian.

"I would like to you to come over and take a look at the two men we have in custody. Perhaps you may recognize them," Alward said.

Jillian nodded. "Of course."

"Follow me." The detective began to walk toward the two police cars that sat without their lights on. Jillian followed, then turned to look at Ian.

He gestured for her to continue. "I'm right behind you."

Jillian jogged a few yards to catch up to the detective who'd slowed down so that she could catch up.

"If you know who they are, please let us know," Alward replied. "Please open the back door so Ms. Connors can see the men inside."

The uniformed policeman went over and opened the driver's side of the patrol car. The cabin flooded with light. Jillian stopped and peered inside. The man had black hair that was cut so short that it was more bald than not.

The man's eyes clamped shut as he reacted to the brightness. Slowly, over the course of a few seconds, he gradually began to open them. He glanced back at the officer with wariness and then his gaze lighted on her. Curiosity registered in his eyes as he studied her. Jillian crossed her arms and shook her head. "No. I don't know this man."

She looked over at the detective and discovered that he had been studying her reaction as she looked at the man in the car. Now she knew why she'd been told to stay away from the squad cars. She was still under suspicion. Any hint that she recognized them would have probably been damning.

Jillian cast a quick glance over to Ian who stood back in silence. His attention floated between the man in the car, the detective, and then finally back to her. He shook his head. "I don't recognize him either."

Detective Alward shut the car door. "Maybe you know the other one."

He escorted them to the second vehicle and opened the door. The vehicle's inside lit up, and in the back seat Jillian spied another man. The man was clad in jeans and a dark t-shirt and appeared to be deliberately looking away from the open door. Dark copper hair, lean build. Unease rose within her. She leaned in closer to get a better look and gasped.

"Wesley?"

CHAPTER TWENTY-FIVE

Ian sank down into the chair and set the water bottle down. Jillian had been with the detectives for over two hours, and if he had to wait much longer, he was on the edge of going flat-out nuts. What could be taking so long?

Jillian had been so insistent that she didn't need to bring a lawyer, but Ian wasn't so sure that was the best of ideas. She'd clearly been the wronged party in this whole mess, but he frankly wasn't so confident the detectives saw it that way. With her brother disappearing for several days and then hiding drugs in his sister's business, Ian suspected the detectives thought it all looked a little too convenient.

His cell phone pinged. He checked his text messages. One from Shawn. *Any news?*

Ian exhaled, leaned back in the chair, and texted a reply. *Not yet.*

Last night after the police had left, Jillian began to make phone calls, to her parents, her sister, and an attorney that handled criminal cases. Ian would be willing to bet a dinner at the best steak restaurant in town that Wesley would not get off with a round of probation and some rehab this time. Drug running, especially meth, pretty well ensured that they would be sending him to prison for a number of years.

Jillian knew that too. He saw it in the intensity of how she made one call after another, with no guilt at calling everyone and dragging people out of bed. She was like a bulldog working on a bone, never letting go. Kind of reminded him of his brother. Shawn could be relentless.

Ian rubbed his face and surveyed the room. Definitely your basic bare bones situation. Rows of plastic chairs were claimed by people sitting in clusters of two to three. They didn't look at each other and seemed to be focusing on their own circumstances as they talked and checked their cell phones.

He could use at least one good night's sleep, but he could do without the nightmares. His brother was right. It was time to seek help.

The door on the other end of the waiting area opened and Jillian walked through. She looked about as bad as he felt. She walked directly over to him and into his open arms.

He felt her exhale and soften as if all the tension in her body dialed back a notch after a few moments. "Jilli. I'm sorry."

He wished he could think of something better to say. His comment was a weak platitude, but right now it was the best he could offer.

She pulled back, looking him in the eyes. "I was right."

Huh, right? His face must have registered the "what are you talking about look" because she said, "About Wes. I was right. He isn't using drugs. The drug screen came back clean, and he said he wasn't using drugs."

Oh dear God, not that again. Ian struggled to find the words that would ensure his reply didn't escalate the conversation to World War III.

"Okay.… What has he been up to?"

Jillian glanced around the seating area. "We need to talk somewhere private."

Ian nodded. "Got it. Do you want something to eat? Go get coffee? Or?"

"I don't care. Just let's get out of here. I'm starving. What time is it?"

"Close to eleven," Ian replied.

"I could use something to eat. Anywhere will do."

"I came down Central Avenue. Around Thomas, I thought I saw an International House of Pancakes."

Jillian shifted her purse to her other shoulder. "Perfect."

Ian gently touched her arm and guided her out of the waiting room. They headed to the parking lot. Every few strides, he cast a glance over at Jillian, trying to get a read on what she was thinking. Finally, he broke the silence. "Are you okay?"

"I'm fine. Wesley will be fine."

Whoa! Did she just say that Wesley would be fine? What kind of fantasy was she clinging to? He pressed his lips together and continued to walk the block to the car. Finally when they got to his car, Ian couldn't stand it any longer.

"Okay, spill it."

"Wesley hadn't relapsed. He wasn't using drugs," she stated flatly.

"Then what…"

She looked across at Ian. Exhaustion hung on her face. "Remember when we talked to Wes's friends and they talked about the times they did the boys night out and went to the casinos?"

For a fleeting second, Ian's train of thought stopped. Where was this going? "Um, yeah."

"I got a chance to talk to Wesley. He said that he started gambling. A little here and there, but then things escalated, and it got expensive. Wes was gambling mostly on sports events, and he blew through most of his inheritance at the casinos. He would disappear and gamble during the work week for an hour or two here and there, but eventually, when most of the money was gone, he found other ways to place bets. He placed bets with bookies. Is that what they are called?"

"I believe so," Ian added.

"Anyway, in some cases, they will extend credit. He applied. No, let me correct that statement. Thanks to Wesley, I applied for credit. He used my information. That's how Rossi knew so much about me and my business. I was the good credit risk, and Wes wasn't."

Jillian's eyes watered and her chin trembled. "Oh Ian, you should have heard him talk. Wes believes he can win it all back, even now. He said he'd pay off the loan when he wins. He's so disconnected. It's as if he doesn't realize how serious this is."

Ian stared. Well, he'd not seen that one coming. Gambling. "So if he's not into drugs, how did he end up trafficking them?"

Jillian shook her head and softly snorted a laugh. "You were right. Because signing over his BMW only covered part of the loan amount he'd taken with Rossi, and the rest he worked off by trans-porting and storing them."

Ian ran his hand through his hair. "Jillian, I'm glad Wes hasn't started using drugs again, but I've got to be honest here. This looks worse for him."

She shook her head. "No, it's going to be okay." Jillian raised her hands up to her face, covered her eyes, and took a slightly ragged breath.

"How?" Ian asked.

"Because the police want Rossi. They want him badly."

The hum of a car's engine echoed from the floor above and grew louder. Ian cast a glance in the car's direction and watched as it continued to the lower level of the parking garage.

"Oh, man."

Chewing on her lower lip, Jillian crossed her arms. "What?"

"If Wesley talks, his life is in danger."

"But…"

"No, Jilli, hear me out. Rossi has evaded law enforcement for a long time. He's dirty and dangerous. Look at what information Wesley can reveal. Drugs, gambling, identity theft, and possible loan sharking. Do you think a man of that character is going to simply let Wesley blow the lid off things?"

She blinked and then the blood leached from her face.

"Please tell me that the police, the DEA, or whomever is crafting this deal, has some plans to keep him safe up to and after the trial."

"I don't know," Jillian whispered.

"Who is Wesley making this deal with? Phoenix PD?"

"Honestly, Ian, I don't know. Most of the time Wesley just

talked about what happened and how he was going to make a deal. I was so shocked and then relieved that I just let him go on."

She began to sway. Ian steadied her and shuttled her over to the passenger side of the car.

"Sit," he growled as he unlocked the passenger side and settled her into the seat.

"I have to contact Wesley's attorney."

"Yes, you do. But right now, first things first. You need to get some food in you." He held the passenger side door open as she pivoted in the seat and pulled her legs in. Ian pressed his lips tightly together as her skirt rode up slightly, revealing a bit more of her shapely legs.

"I think some pancakes are in order. IHOP it is."

Jillian groaned. "I don't think that I could eat anything now." .

"Try," Ian urged. "You're going to need to keep your strength up."

With that, he closed the door and marched around the back of the car to the driver's side. His cell phone pinged and he glanced at the text message.

Any news?

He stopped and typed a quick reply to Shawn. *And then some. Will call later.*

CHAPTER TWENTY-SIX

Jillian sank back into the passenger seat. *Wesley is still in danger.* She swung down the visor and flipped up the lid to reveal the mirror. Her hair, pulled tight in a ponytail, only made her pale complexion and ever-darkening circles under her eyes look more noticeable.

Given that she had not had a good night's sleep in days, she had every right to look like she'd been run through the wringer. She watched Ian as he stopped behind the car and checked his phone. He quickly punched a short reply and then continued over to the driver's side door.

He opened the door, slid into the driver's seat, and began to fasten his seat belt. She watched in silence. What would she have done without him? When he had first walked into the room a few days back, Jillian had been stunned. She'd not heard anything about Ian being back. For all she knew, Ian was still in the Army and could be deployed again. Thank God, he'd come home in one piece. At least physically. His mental and emotional state was another matter entirely. He had finally opened up and let her know what was at the source of the recurring nightmares that had been taking place.

Ian prided himself of being strong and able to handle things, but in regard to coming to terms with the loss of his friend, he needed some help. The question was, would he seek it?

He moved forward to insert the key into the ignition and she touched his forearm. "Hey. Did I ever say how much I appreciate that you've been there with me through all of this?"

A look of concern washed across his features. "Jillian…"

"No." She placed her finger gently to his lips. "I have to say this before I lose my nerve. Ian, I don't know how I would have gotten through all of this without you being by my side. I know that we parted ways long ago, and when this case is done you have every right to move on, but…"

Jillian paused. Did she dare say it? That she still loved him. That there had been no one else since him? She swallowed the lump in her throat. "Just thank you," she whispered.

She pulled her hand back and Ian clasped it. "You're not getting rid of me that easily this time." He gently traced his other hand along her cheek and jawline, then stopped near her lips. He paused only for a few brief seconds before he kissed her.

The kiss was soft and slow as if he savored every facet of her. Jillian inhaled and softly moaned. The faint scent of his aftershave drifted to her. Dark, musky. The heat of his breath, and his lips, soft yet persistent, coaxed her for more. She gently eased backward and waited a couple of seconds before opening her eyes.

Relief, giddiness, and the full-on urge to do much more than kiss coursed through her like a buzz of electricity. *How can something that felt so right be the wrong thing to do right now?* "I need to take things slow and be sure we both don't hurt each other again. Everything has been happening so quickly. Let's not hurry into something before we're ready. "

Hurt flickered in his eyes and he broke eye contact, pulled back, and leaned into the driver's seat. "Yeah, you're right."

He turned on the ignition. As he shifted the car into reverse, he glanced over at her. "I'll give you time to figure this out. But I know what I want, and it's you, Jillian, and this time I'm not going to leave you."

Ian didn't wait for her to answer, but turned on the radio and pulled out of the parking space.

"Off for brunch," he added quietly.

***

"Well?" Shawn Randall looked up from his desk as Ian stood in the doorway.

"Do you want the good news or the bad news first?" Ian asked.

"Oh, no." Shawn gestured for his brother to come into his office.

Ian sank into the chair in front of his brother's desk and stretched his legs out in front of him. "Would you like to take a guess as to what caused Wesley to make a run for it?"

"Drugs?"

"Nope. They're involved, but they aren't the primary reason why Wesley committed identity theft, stole from his sister, and transported drugs."

Shawn locked eyes with him. "Don't keep me in suspense any longer."

"Gambling," Ian replied. "Wesley has a gambling addiction."

Shawn's eyes widened in shock. "You're kidding."

"Nope. Seems like things started innocently enough. Just the guys going to the casinos, having a few drinks, doing a little gambling, and for Wes, it escalated."

Shawn began to fiddle with a pen on his desk. "Damn," he whispered as he shook his head. "How is Jillian handling it?"

Ian snorted a soft laugh. "Relieved and worried, if that's possible at the same time. Relieved he didn't relapse and start using drugs, worried because they now have a new addiction that must be addressed."

"Not angry? I mean, the guy stole from her, forged her name on a loan, and set her up in the sights of a drug dealer."

"Oh I think anger will come, eventually. Right now she's trying to find some balance and stay up-to-date with all the communication between family, the attorney and her brother," Ian answered. "And, Wes told her that he's going to make a deal and expose Rossi for his role in all of this."

Shawn sighed. "Why doesn't that surprise me?"

"Well it sure knocked Jilli for a loop. When he told her that, she just rolled with it. It wasn't until after we talked that she had even considered that being a witness for the prosecution would put Wesley in danger." Ian paused. "She never thought to ask who Wesley was cutting the deal with, and what their plans are to keep him safe."

Shawn crooked a small grin at Ian. "Jilli? You haven't called her that in years."

Ian flashed a smile. "There is no getting anything past you, is there?"

"So?" Shawn asked.

"We're taking things slow and see how they develop," Ian replied.

"Fair enough."

"Oh, God no," Ian whispered.

"What?"

"What if Rossi gets wind of what Wesley is going to do? If he can't get to Wes, he may try for Jillian. He had no problems trashing her car to make a point. She could be used as leverage." He glanced at his brother. *Come on, Shawn, please tell me that I'm overreacting and that this case is closed. Tell me the woman I love is not in danger anymore.*

"Where is Jillian?"

"At the office. She had paperwork and said that she needed to make calls to everyone as to what had happened this morning."

"Check in. Keep an eye on her," Shawn said.

Ian nodded, rose from the chair and began to walk to the door.

"Ian."

He paused, hand on the doorknob.

"Take all the time you need to make sure she's safe," Shawn added.

He delivered one single nod. "Thanks."

CHAPTER TWENTY-SEVEN

Once in the hall, Ian grabbed his cell phone. When he called Jillian, he only got her voice mail. He didn't leave a message, but then tried her private office number.

"Come on, Jilli, answer." He growled as he picked up his pace and headed for the front entrance. A busy signal registered, and Ian sighed. Not as good as talking to her, but good enough to know that she was still at the office and on the phone with someone. The voice mailbox greeting came on. He strode through the front lobby and out the entrance of Sonoran Security. The phone beeped. "Jilli. Ian. Don't leave the office. Lock the door. I'm on my way, and call me when you get this message."

He sucked in a deep breath of the warm desert air as he strode across the outdoor courtyard and toward the parking lot. The heat registered on his face and down his throat. Ian picked up the pace as he exited the courtyard and entered the air-conditioned lobby.

He stopped and gripped his phone and stared across the marble floor and out the glass doors of the building complex entrance. He glanced around. *Good. No one's here.* Ian closed his eyes and images floated into his head. The plain white buildings, heat, and the neutral tan of his uniform. Ian opened his eyes. *Not in Iraq. In Scottsdale. Jillian needs me.* He focused on the cars outside in the parking lot and consciously slowed his breathing. *In. Hold your breath and exhale slowly.* The nervous electricity receded. *Again.* He inhaled and exhaled several more times until he couldn't feel the anxiety any more. "Good. Real good," he whispered. He fished out his keys and slowly walked to the glass doors at the front of the building.

Ian clicked his key fob as he approached his car to unlock the doors and as he slid in, he set the phone on the holder to the right of the driver's side. He turned on the motor and looked at the time, which came upon the car console. It had been only five minutes, but it felt like twenty. He picked up his cell phone as he considered calling her again.

No, the voice in his head said, give her another five to ten minutes. Setting the phone down, he backed the car out of the covered parking place and pulled out onto the street. If he made the lights, he could be there in twenty minutes.

***

"Done," she whispered, setting the handset down on the phone and leaning back in her chair

She rubbed her forehead. It had taken some time, but she'd finally completed making all the calls and now everyone was up to speed on all of what had transpired. Her sister, Shelby, was actually more concerned about Jillian.

"How are you holding up?" Shelby asked.

"Fine. I'm fine," Jillian replied, and then she finally revealed that for the past few days she been over at Ian's apartment until they could be sure that she was in no danger from Rossi.

Jillian sensed her sister was not happy about the fact that they'd reconnected. However, after she told her what Ian had said earlier today in the car, her sister warmed up a bit to his return in her life.

"I'm just concerned for you. It sounds as if he'll need to get some help with the nightmares and the flashbacks. Oh Jillian, I can't imagine what he's seen and been through. I want the best for Ian, but—"

"I understand." Jillian cut her sister off. "But we'll work our way through all of this. We have to."

Jillian disconnected the call, dropped her handset to her lap, and then remembered she'd never told her sister that she knew, deep in her bones, that she loved Ian. Shelby, who'd told Ian she'd moved on, and had been with her when Jillian discovered that he enlisted was gone. Her sister wasn't ready to hear that this time their relationship would survive all this mess. No yet.

She glanced over at the phone and noticed the message light was lit. Jillian punched in the password to retrieve the message. Ian's worry came through when she heard him speak her name. "Stay in the office. Lock the door. Call me." He issued instructions as if they were orders.

Jillian deleted the message and began to dial his number as she stood up and walked over and locked the door to her office.

"Jillian?"

"Hey. I'm fine. What happened?"

She heard him exhale. "What do you know about this so-called plea deal Wesley is negotiating? Have you got any information from his attorney?" Ian asked.

"Nothing more than what Wes told me this morning when we talked. I spoke to his attorney earlier and he was very tight-lipped. Didn't even confirm or deny there was a potential deal in the works. He told me the less I knew the better, because I might be deposed."

"So in your opinion, is there a deal or isn't there?"

Jillian sank back into her chair. "Honestly, Ian, I don't know." She raked her fingers through her hair and swept the strands away from her face. "Wesley thinks there is one on the table. If that helps."

Ian didn't comment for several seconds. Finally, Jillian broke the silence. "Ian, what's wrong?"

"I can't say with one hundred percent certainty, but Shawn agrees with me that if Wesley's attorney is in fact crafting a plea deal, Rossi may use you to apply leverage to make Wesley not talk about what has happened."

Leverage. The word jumped out at her. The drug dealer had a lot to lose if Wesley testified.

"But I just moved back to my place. What am I supposed to do? Hide? Stay with you again?"

"You're safer with me."

Jillian bit her lip. *Just how exactly am I supposed to respond to that?* Part of her didn't like the answer or Ian acting all Tarzan. And yet, at some other level, there was this girly side of her who kind of got a little giddy hearing it.

"Where are you?" Jillian asked.

"On my way over to your office." Ian replied. "What's on the schedule for the remainder of the day?"

"Not much. I booked a couple of tours on next Monday. We're starting to see people look at us for fall and winter weddings."

"I thought June was the wedding month."

"It is, for the most part. But with our climate, fall and winter weddings are also quite popular. I've got another wedding here in a week. So, to be honest, I am praying that this goes back to normal soon."

The phone went dead for a few moments and Jillian wondered if his cell had the lost connection.

"Normal," Ian whispered. "What a wonderful idea. I've forgotten what that feels like."

Jillian smiled. "I suspect when things get to normal, you'll get bored."

Ian laughed softly. "I'd like to have an opportunity to deal with that. What do you want to do for dinner tonight?"

"How about if we crash and I fix something? I make a mean chicken and rice casserole. How does that sound?"

"Sounds great. Be there in ten minutes."

CHAPTER TWENTY-EIGHT

Jillian dropped her purse on the dining room table and set the pet carrier on the ground. "Let me get changed into something more comfortable and I'll get dinner started."

Ian nodded as he carried the bag of groceries to the kitchen. "Go ahead and I'll put this stuff in the fridge."

She bent down, opened the door, and let her cat exit the carrier when he chose. Jillian slowly walked around the corner of the kitchen and leaned a hip against the counter.

Ian glanced up from unpacking the plastic bags and asked. "What?"

Jillian waved her hand in the air. "Never mind. I'll be back in a few minutes. Simon, cut Ian some slack."

She slid her hand down his back and stopped to scratch the area just above the tail. Simon arched his back and meowed. "You understand me, don't you?"

The cat closed his eyes and purred loudly. Jillian straightened, then hurried into the bedroom.

With the door closed, she slipped out of her dress and heels and changed into a pair of cropped pants and a cotton top. She paused briefly to look in the mirror to check things out. She straightened the shirt and tucked her hair behind her ears. She felt the tension of the day loosen a bit, and her shoulders felt as if a load had been removed. For a brief few moments, the fear for her brother and the concerns for his safety had ebbed. All she was thinking about was getting dinner in the oven and having a nice relaxing evening with Ian.

For days, the nagging doubt that when this case was over Ian would leave and she'd never hear from him again had been lingering in her thoughts. Yet, this morning he had told her he wasn't leaving this time. She saw it in his eyes. He was telling the truth. Now if Ian could just find some peace about Iraq.

She couldn't even begin to imagine what it had been like to stand there and watch one of your best friends get hit by a car. Not an accident, but a deliberate and calculated act to kill someone.

She knew him well enough to know that he was desperately trying to fight and hide the fear that he was possibly losing his mind. She suspected Shawn wasn't blind to what was happening. But when Ian had disclosed earlier today that Shawn had suggested Ian seek some counseling, she knew that Ian may have finally arrived at the tipping point and recognized that he needed help.

Jillian left the bedroom and went to the kitchen. Ian had removed his tie and jacket and opened the bottle of Pinot Grigio and pulled two wine glasses out of the cabinet. "Do you want your wine on ice?"

She smiled. "You remembered."

Ian picked up a glass, opened the freezer, and dropped a few cubes in a glass. "I remember a lot."

He poured the wine and handed her the glass. She noted that the amounts he'd poured into the two glasses looked equal and were about one third full. *Good. He's not power drinking.* She took a sip as he did the same.

He took a large sip and set the glass down. "It's my turn to get into something more comfortable."

"Sounds good. I'll get the casserole started."

When he started to walk past her, suddenly Jillian softly clasped his arm. He turned to her with puzzled eyes.

"I just want to say thank you again," she murmured.

The corners of his lips turned up. Then before she let go, he leaned in and planted a soft kiss. Without any further comment, he turned and headed back into the bedroom to change. Jillian stood there and felt the warmth fade as he walked away. Her eyes lit on the cat, who must have sat there and watched her and Ian.

"Well, what do you think?" she asked softly.

The Siamese didn't respond, but turned and followed Ian.

Jillian's cell phone rang. She pulled it out of her purse and without a second thought she answered call.

"Good evening, Jillian."

She gasped. *Rossi.* "What do you want?"

"Oh, I think you know," the man replied. "Rumor has it that someone is talking to the authorities about me and that is not a good idea."

Jillian's mouth went dry, and she swallowed. "I don't know anything about a deal."

"Maybe not. But you need to let your brother know that if he talks, there will be a price to be paid."

Jillian didn't say anything. She was not sure how to respond to this. Ian walked around the corner and stopped. His expression darkened.

"Rossi," Jillian mouthed.

He gestured to have her hand the phone over to him. Jillian moved closer so that he could hear, but Ian firmly removed it from her grasp.

"Leave us alone," he growled. "Leave Jillian alone. She doesn't know anything about Wesley's so-called deal. If there is any deal, Wesley's attorney is not talking. They've completely left us in the dark."

Seconds ticked by and just when she thought he'd hung up, Rossi spoke, "Jillian, remember what I said and let your brother know."

The line went silent. "He's disconnected."

"Damn it!" Ian shouted. "I was afraid this would happen."

"What do we do?"

Ian handed Jillian's phone back to her, and then paced back and forth in the living room area before stopping. "We must contact Wesley, his attorney, and the police. They need to know that Rossi knows. And we need to get the hell out of here, as soon as possible."

"But..."

"No buts. How Rossi found out about this, I have no clue. Maybe he has an informant somewhere in the jail. Maybe Wesley isn't as safe as everybody thinks in a solitary cell. Right now all we have is a string of maybes, but I know this if he wants to get his point across, all he has to do is hurt you, Shelby, or even your parents."

Ian grabbed his cell phone. "I'm calling Shawn. We need to find a safe place to hide. Do you have Wesley's lawyer's phone number?"

"I have the office number. It's after hours, though."

Ian nodded. "Call the office and leave a message to have them call back. In the meantime, let's get packing. We're moving. Even Simon is coming."

Chapter Twenty-Nine

Jillian looked out the passenger side window as they traveled down the small, almost single lane road. Ian had slowed the car to a speed which would have been appropriate for a school zone and that was a good thing. They had left the paved asphalt a couple of minutes ago and they were driving on a scraped dirt road. Lights off to the right and left of the road indicated houses were out in the desert, but they were tucked so far off the road they must be on large parcels of land.

"So, who is Stella?" she asked.

"Matt's fiancé," Ian replied. "A few months back, she hired him to provide construction on her house flip, and the rest, as they say, is history. They are going to put us up at her place."

Ian looked over, or at least she thought he did in the darkness of the car's cabin. "I think you'll like her."

"'Okay."

Lord, I hope so. When Ian called for a secure place to move to, never in my wildest dreams would Matt suggest they stick them on a horse-property tucked away in North Scottsdale.

As they neared a turn in the road, a large Spanish-style arch indicated the entrance to a property. "Here we go," Ian said.

Slowly he pulled through the gate and paused as if he wasn't sure where to go next.

"There." Jillian pointed to a truck that was parked next to a barn with fenced runs coming from each of the stalls.

"Stella lives here?" Jillian asked.

"No, this is a flip. Once finished, she plans to put it on the market. They plan to ask a lot for it."

"Obviously." Jillian glanced around and from what she could see from the barn lights and the moonlight, a new house was nearing the end stages of construction. Ahead she could make out a fence in the darkness and to the right, a large barn with fencing allowing the horses to access a run from each stall door.

As they neared, Matt walked out to greet them and a tall blond woman came and stood by his side. Bathed in the light from the car beams, all Jillian could think was that they made a striking couple.

Ian parked the car and turned off the engine. "Okay, let's go see our new digs." He opened the door and stepped out. Jillian followed suit.

"Rossi should have a hard time following us here. We're so off the grid, I'm sure I don't have cell phone reception," Jillian remarked.

The woman's soft laughter drifted toward them.

"You've got reception. Believe it or not, there is a cell phone tower less than a mile away from here," Matt answered.

Matt gently placed his hand in the small of the blonde woman's back. "Jillian, meet my fiancée, Stella Adams."

The woman extended her hand. "Hi, nice to meet you."

"Nice to meet you too. Thanks for putting us up here."

Stella smiled. "My pleasure. Anything to help Ian." She cast a quick glance over at Ian and then back to Jillian.

"I've talked with Matt. The house is finished, but doesn't have any furniture in it yet, but the apartment off the barn is furnished. So if you don't mind being around horses, this might be a more comfortable place to stay."

"You have horses here?"

"You're not selling this place?" Ian asked.

Stella and Matt looked at each other and cracked a smile almost in unison.

"Change of plans," Matt said.

"Stella and I are selling our places and moving here. Seems like my wife-to-be has decided that she wants to own, ride, and breed Arabian horses."

Jillian noted that Matt had emphasized the breed part of that statement.

Stella laughed. "Don't believe I'm dragging Matt into this against his will. It was his idea." She paused for a second and looked into Matt's eyes before leaning into him as he slid his arm over her shoulder. "There's a cowboy under all those professional business suits."

The tall Texan leaned over and planted a kiss on her cheek, and then glanced back at Jillian and Ian. "Come on, let's get you moved in and then we'll give you a small tour."

Jillian took a quick peek over at Ian, who crooked a grin

at her. Matt gestured to Ian's car. "Need a hand getting the stuff moved in?"

"Yes, please," Jillian replied.

Matt and Stella separated and started walking to the car, and Jillian uttered a silent prayer that they wouldn't panic when they saw what she'd managed to stuff into Ian's car. In addition to suitcases, a cat and related equipment, she'd also brought food as well. She wasn't sure how long they would have to stay in hiding. If it was for any period of time, any food in the fridge at Ian's apartment would have gone bad, so she had persuaded Ian to bring that along.

Ian walked around to the trunk, opened it, and he and Matt pulled out the suitcases.

"What's that in the back seat?" Stella asked.

"Simon. My cat. I'm guessing he's hunkered down in the back of the carrier. This is the second move he's taken within a week."

Stella peered into the container. "He's pretty. Siamese?"

"Yes. Normally he's a bit chatty. Siamese usually are, but recently he's been quiet."

"Well, the sun room off the side of the apartment should be of interest to him. With all the wildlife out there, he should have lots of things to look at. I'm betting he'll probably find the quail fascinating. Just be careful to keep him indoors. We do have coyote, snakes, and bobcats."

"Thanks for letting me know," Jillian replied.

"Why don't you bring him in, and I'll bring the food, litter pan, and then we'll make one more trip to bring in the rest," Stella added.

Jillian smiled. Ian was right. She liked Stella. The woman had an easy-going air about her.

Ian and Matt were walking the dirt path up to the side entrance of the barn.

Jillian held the cat carrier and waited as Stella removed the items from the back seat. As she rearranged the items to carry them more easily, Stella glanced up and noted Matt and Ian had disappeared into the barn. "So, how is Ian doing?"

Jillian paused. Stella had phrased the question so matter-of-factly that she almost missed the note of concern.

"Pretty well. He has nightmares. Don't let him know I've told you that."

Stella nodded. "He's been through a lot and isn't willing to talk about it. Matt said that Shawn is worried."

"He finally opened up a bit last night. He saw one of his friends get killed. What else he's been through, God only knows."

"He's talking to you?"

"Yeah. Not a whole lot, but I've discovered if you push him, he tends to shut down."

Jillian circled around to Stella's side. "Not sure I'm qualified to help him deal with all this," Stella said. "I mean, I'm not a psychologist or something. Sounds like he is taking the first step by talking to someone. That's the most important part. You knew each other from before this case, right?"

"Yes," Jillian said. "We screwed things up the first time. So, we're taking things slowly."

Stella glanced over and Jillian could see from the expression in the tall blond's face that she approved of what Jillian had just said. Stella smiled. "If we can provide any help. You only have to ask."

"Thanks," Jillian said.

The two women walked up the dirt path that led to the side entrance of the barn. Jillian slowed and let Stella take the lead. After a short distance they went into the side door of an apartment. As they stepped inside Jillian followed across the den area and set the pet carrier with Simon on the floor. Stella stacked the assortment of cat supplies on the small stool tucked under the breakfast bar that faced into a partially open galley kitchen.

The floor had Saltillo tile and a large Persian-style area rug defined the seating area, which consisted of a sofa, end tables, a coffee table and a recliner on one side. All the furniture faced a wall which was floor-to-ceiling with shelves for books and a large flat screen TV that was mounted in the center for easy viewing.

"Oh, this is lovely. When you said it was attached to the barn, I wasn't sure what to expect."

Stella laughed. "Something a little more on the 'rustic' side, right?"

"I'm a little embarrassed to admit it, but..." She paused and cracked a nervous grin. "Yes, I was thinking we're were going to have to rough it a bit."

"It's a one-bedroom unit, suitable for one person or perhaps a couple. I thought it would work for a property manager or caretaker. Or, we might even rent it out as an efficiency apartment." Stella looked at the kitchen. "I'm afraid there isn't a lot of extra space in here. Would putting the litter box in the bathroom work?"

"That will be fine. In fact, if we placed it anywhere else, I'm not sure Simon would know where to find it."

"Follow me." Stella leaned over and picked up the litter pan and bag of kitty litter and walked through a door just off the kitchen. "Bathroom is on the right." She flipped on the switch and stepped back so Jillian could take a look.

The bathroom was done in earth tones. A large shower, with a rainforest style nozzle and nearly invisible glass walls stood in the back, double sinks graced a dark storage cabinet, and tucked behind a privacy wall was a toilet.

Jillian laughed. "Definitely not going to be roughing it."

Stella grinned, then set the litter pan down in the corner of the bathroom and gestured to Jillian. "Come on, let me show you the rest."

Stella led her down a short hall and into the bedroom. "Voilá."

The room had a large bed, a dresser, an armoire, and night tables. Jillian forced a smile. Stella may have assumed that they were sharing a bed, something she and Ian would have to figure something out, discreetly, after they left tonight.

The Southwest decorating theme had been continued with the furniture being dark, heavy wood. A large Navajo rug softened the ceramic tile.

Stella opened the armoire. "A TV on the top shelf. We have satellite dish hookup so you can pretty much watch whatever you want."

To the right, sliding doors indicated the closet and to the left a large sliding barn door could be opened to the sun room. Jillian walked over to the doorway and looked out. It was dark and the city lights glittered in the distance.

"Wow, Stella, thank you so much for offering this as a place to hide out."

She turned to Jillian and gently touched her arm. "No problem. I think you'll be safe here. Forgive me if this seems a little pushy, but Ian's a good guy and I'm glad you two have found each other again."

"Me too."

"I don't know if you had a chance to have any dinner, but I stocked the fridge with some food. It's not fancy, just some sliced meats, cheeses. You can make sandwiches. Come, let's find the guys."

Jillian expected they might have crashed on the sofa after bringing in the last of the items from the car, but it looked like they'd stashed the food from the car in the fridge and had disappeared.

After a couple minutes of searching, she and Stella found them in the barn aisle talking, and Matt was petting a horse which had stuck its head over the Dutch door.

"Thought I would find you here," Stella said as she and Jillian entered the barn and walked down the dirt corridor to the stall the men stood by.

Ian grinned and gestured to Jillian. "Come here and meet our roommate."

Jillian paused for a fraction of a second before following Stella down the aisle. "I've never been around horses."

Stella laughed. "Funny, I said the same thing about six months ago."

CHAPTER THIRTY

Jillian glanced down at the time on her cell phone and frowned. "We're going to be late for Wes' arraignment," Jillian whispered.

"Sorry. I had no idea downtown traffic would be this bad," Ian responded. "If it'll help, let me drop you off. You can go into the court building and I'll park the car and catch up with you."

Jillian glanced over at Ian, who gripped the steering wheel with white knuckles. Guilt nibbled at her. He was navigating through the traffic the best he could. A car cut in front of them and then quickly came to a near stop as it angled a turn to get into a side street.

"Oh come on, buddy," Ian muttered. "You're killing us here."

Jillian laid her hand on his arm. "Relax."

"It's all these one-way streets in downtown around the government buildings and the courthouse. I don't know who thought this was a good idea, but clearly...."

"There," Jillian gestured to the building on the right. "If you can make a quick stop somewhere near there I can walk the rest of the distance."

"Got it," Ian replied. Within seconds he had maneuvered across two lanes of traffic and pulled to a stop.

Jillian stepped out, and then leaned down and looked back at Ian. "Just a reminder. No firearms allowed in the courthouse."

"I know. Hurry or you'll miss Wesley."

Jillian closed the car door and slung her purse over her shoulder. She walked briskly toward the building's front entrance. From the corner of her eye, she saw Ian drive the car past her and down the street. She threaded her way through the people, nearly colliding with a homeless man who stood in the crowd holding a sign claiming he was a vet and soliciting money.

Another one that has fallen through the cracks. Jillian's gut tightened as the gaunt man with the well-worn clothes looked away from her and on to another person in hopes of a donation. She climbed up the steps to the courthouse entrance as the memory of last night returned.

Ian had another episode. He'd slept in the recliner. As she'd heard muffled noise from the den, she'd jolted from a deep sleep.

Ian had tossed and flailed his arms as he drew ragged draws of air. *No, not again. When will he have some peace?* She considered if she should try to wake him. The last time she'd tried to wake him, she'd learned the hard way that Ian was still in 'battle mode' when the nightmares came, and she had the bruises to show for it. Did she dare try again?

He seemed to calm down as his arm dropped from the arm rest. Jillian's gut tightened. She had to do something to help. She slowly walked toward him. "Ian. It's me. Jilli. It's okay. You're here with me. Breathe, Ian. You're not in Iraq, but in Phoenix."

Ian stilled and Jillian stopped a few steps short of the man. She watched and waited. He was still breathing rapidly. *What was he reliving? A battle?*

Jillian took another step. "Ian, relax. Hey babe, it's me. I'm here at home, come back to me." She touched his shoulder. He was rock solid and tense, like an animal ready to spring.

"Ian, you're home." Slowly she slid her hand down his arm. His hands, clenched in tight knots, softened. Jillian didn't speak but continued to rub his arm softly. *Ian, when will your torment end? Come home to me, not just in body, but in heart and mind.*

Slowly, moment by moment, his fists opened and the muscles relaxed under her touch. His breathing slowed to normal. *Better, much better.*

Jillian pulled her hand back, stood up, and turned to walk back to the bedroom. Just before she left the room, she turned and looked back at him. He was awake.

"Nightmare?" Jillian asked.

Ian nodded.

"Go back to sleep." She turned and walked to the bedroom and before she closed the door, she could have sworn she heard Ian say. "Love you too, babe."

Jillian checked her cell phone as she waited in line to clear the security checks. Adrenaline hummed through her. "Dear God, I hope that Wes isn't grasping for some kind of pipe dream, in regards to making a deal," she murmured.

Shelby texted. *Has the arraignment started?* Jillian quickly punched in a reply. *Don't know. Traffic was nasty. Running late, on my way to his courtroom.* After tossing the phone into her purse, she set it down on the tray and positioned it to roll down and get scanned via X-ray. She slowly walked through the metal detector and then picked up her purse on the other end.

Picking up the pace, she arrived just in time to squeeze into an upward-bound elevator and as they stopped on floor after floor, Jillian watched the expressions on the people who exited.

The emotions went the gamut from resignation to hopefulness. Finally the door opened on the floor she was waiting for, and she stepped out. Within a minute she'd located the room, slid in the back door, and dropped into a chair.

Small groups of people sat in clusters on benches spaced in the courtroom. The door opened behind her and in came Wesley's attorney.

"Mr. Greene? I'm Jillian. Wesley's sister."

The lawyer was lean, almost skinny, with grey hair a couple shades lighter than the expensive suit he wore.

"Ms. Connors."

"The traffic was horrible. I was concerned that Wes had been arraigned already."

"No. His case is after this one that is starting now." The attorney tilted his head to the front of the room and Jillian watched a woman in an orange jumpsuit be escorted into the room.

"Just a reminder. This should be short, your brother will be charged. Bail, if any, will be set."

The attorney started to walk up to the first row and Jillian grabbed her purse and followed him.

"Don't speak to your brother or even approach him. Given the nature of the charges, bail will be high."

The nervous hum amped up to a full-blown gut-wrenching buzz. "Okay."

Greene stopped at the first row and indicated that she take a seat. Jillian took the second seat row and Greene sat down beside her.

Jillian stared at the woman, who stood silently while the charges were presented.

Greene leaned over and whispered, "Your brother has been cooperative and the plan is to let him stay in jail. He'll be in a cell by himself. Wesley should be safe from the jail's general population."

"Okay."

She pressed her lips together and clutched her purse which sat in her lap. "How's he doing in jail?"

The attorney laughed so softly Jillian almost didn't catch it. "He's surviving. You'll see soon."

The woman's arraignment done, she was escorted from the room and Greene stood up and walked up to the table immediately in front of Jillian.

A side door opened, and Wesley entered, escorted by an officer. He was in shackles, which rattled softly as he walked and his hands in restraints.

Wesley cast a quick look around the room and lighted on her. His eyes were dull with fear, and he forced a small, tight smile before turning his attention to the judge as he stood beside his attorney.

The conversation between the judge and the attorneys faded as she studied her brother and took in every detail. He'd lost weight, or at least it appeared so, as the jumpsuit hung on him.

The judge's voice cut through her reverie. "Bail has been set for one million five hundred thousand."

Jillian gasped and then clamped her lips together quickly. Even if she wanted to post bail for her brother, there was no way she could come up with the funds. First, she'd have to find a bail bond company willing to write a bond for that amount, and she have would be in a position to pledge monies and/or assets that was equal to the total amount of the bond.

She stared at the back of Wesley's head in the faint hope that if she focused on it hard enough she would be able to read his mind. He stood there calm and composed. Maybe he was resigned to what would come.

Ian walked up to her left and sat down. "One million, five hundred thousand," she whispered to him.

He clasped her hand. "Hang in there."

The police escorted Wesley out a side door. His attorney packed up his paperwork, turned, and spoke to them. "We'll talk outside." He made a nod to the door at the back of the room.

"Okay," Jillian said, as she and Ian rose from their seats and waited for the attorney in the hall.

As he walked up to them and stood next to her, Jillian picked up the subtle scent of cigarettes. No wonder he was so thin. Maybe he subsisted on a diet of cigarettes and caffeine.

"Was the amount for bail on the high side for this type of offense?" Ian asked.

"A bit. But since Wesley is cooperating with the authorities, they want him where they can keep an eye on him. It works for everybody."

"How long before I can meet with by brother?"

"Give them an hour or so to get him transported back to jail."

The attorney looked at his wristwatch. "I'm sorry but I have to be present for another client. Excuse me."

Without further comment, he walked away.

"What do you think?" Jillian asked as she watched Greene walk away from them.

A long pause followed her question, then Ian finally spoke. "Honestly Jillian, I have no idea."

Chapter Thirty-One

Jillian leaned over and whispered in his ear. "So much for Greene's prediction I'd see Wes in an hour or so. How much longer will I have wait?"

Ian leaned back in the chair and stretched his legs. "Hopefully soon."

He noted that Jillian had settled down since they had arrived at the jail. At first she had been fidgety, standing up a few times and even once, pacing a bit. But as the wait time grew, she finally started relax. Patience was not her strong suit, but it was his. With all his years in the military, Ian had opportunity to hone that quality. Everybody thought that in the army you went from one battle to the next. The truth was more of a case of long periods of boredom punctuated by moments of terror.

He had sympathy for Jillian, but in his opinion, Wesley, needed some serious physiological help. Something ate at Jillian's brother, something which he couldn't fathom. Yes, on an intellectual level he could understand being coaxed by college acquaintances into trying some drugs. Hell, he could even understand getting hooked because you underestimated what you were messing with. But to blow through close to three hundred thousand on gambling? Nope, Ian couldn't wrap his mind around an addiction that worked like that.

He shifted in the chair and looked around the room. He studied the people around him. Yep, there were plenty of stories here, all unfolding in one way or another. He stood up, pulled out his cell phone, and looked at the time.

"Connors." The name came across the speaker and both of them looked toward the front desk.

"Showtime," Ian muttered.

Jillian didn't comment, but picked up her purse and walked toward the desk. As she approached, the officer behind the bulletproof shield studied her.

"I'm Jillian Connors. I'm here to visit my brother Wesley."

The officer asked for ID and then glanced at Ian. "Are you her husband?"

Jillian shook her head and laughed softly.

"No, a friend of the family." He gently placed his hand on the small of Jillian's back as the voice in his head added one final comment to the answer he gave the officer.

"Only family members or their attorney can visit the prisoner. You'll have to wait here."

Ian opened his mouth to protest, but caught the dead-pan expression of the officer's face and shut it. There was no use in arguing. The rules would not be bent to accommodate him.

Besides, he'd not seen Wesley in close to ten years. With him at Jillian's side, Wesley might not talk candidly with his sister.

"It's okay. I'll wait until you get back."

Jillian glanced at him. "I hope to get back soon."

For the next few minutes, paperwork was done and then Jillian, for the second time today, went through a security check.

Once Jillian walked through the doors and into the jail, Ian strolled back into the waiting area and sank down into his chair.

"Who are you here to see?"

Ian looked up at an old man who sat across from him. "I'd rather not talk about it."

The smile on the man's lips dialed back a couple levels. "I don't mean to pry. Just trying to be sociable."

Ian exhaled. He'd hated to admit it but his gruff response did make him sound like a jerk. "Sorry. It's just been a very long couple of days. I'm here with a friend who's here to see her brother. What about you?"

"My son," the man replied. "Ross." He extended his hand. "My name is John Ross."

"Ian Randall."

"Why is your son here?" Ian paused, then quickly added, "if you're comfortable talking about it."

Ross exhaled. "Stupid. My son's in here because he was stupid."

Ian cracked a grin. "Great answer. My friend's brother is in here for being stupid too."

"Yeah, my son went out partying with friends last night. Drank a little too much, and then got behind the wheel of a car." The older man looked around the room and surveyed the other people sitting there. "He's a good kid. Never got into trouble before this. Now…" Ross didn't bother to finish the sentence and just shook his head. Exhaustion hung on the older man's face like a heavy coat.

"How long have you waited to see your son?"

He glanced at his watch. "For over three hours."

"We've waited for over two."

"I know. The tall brunette, right?"

Ian nodded. "Jillian. Her name is Jillian."

"Pretty lady. Seems to be nice. Take good care of her."

Ian crooked a small smile. He intended to when this whole mess was over. "I'll do my best."

The front door of the jail opened. Jillian came out at a brisk walk, searching for him. Ian felt his heart start to race. The expression on her face was near panic. He stood up and started to walk to her. Jillian closed the distance by nearly bolting into a run. "He's getting out. He made bail."

"What?"

"They came to get Wes when we were talking. Ian, someone posted bail for Wes. He's being released."

"When?"

Jillian flinched, and he immediately wished he could ask for a do-over. He practically barked the question at her. "Sorry."

Jillian glanced around the room. She looked as if she was searching for someone. She stepped in closer to Ian and whispered, "I don't know for sure. But soon, maybe thirty to forty-five minutes from now." She crossed her arms. "It's them. They want him on the street. My God, Ian, you should have seen the expression on Wesley's face."

Jillian raised her hands, covered her face for a few moments, and then dropped them. "He looked at me and said he's a dead man."

Ian pressed his lips together and pulled out his cell phone. "Okay, we have to put together a plan to get your brother in a safe and secure location until we get this sorted out."

Jillian covered her hand to her trembling lips.

"Jillian."

She didn't respond.

"Jilli?"

The last comment must have registered because she turned her gaze to him. "I need to call Wes's attorney and we need to figure where we can go to keep him alive. The ranch?"

"Ask the officer who checked you in. Find out what the process in when a prisoner makes bail, how long until release, and where they will release him."

She nodded and walked over to the counter. Ian pulled his cell out and began dialing to connect with either Shawn or Matt. He needed a game plan and fast.

***

Ian walked across the parking garage, clicked the lock, and opened the car door. If anything could go wrong, this would be the time. Shawn and Matt did not pick up their calls. He left a text for both of them. By the time Jillian was able to get a time and location for Wesley's release, and after speaking to his attorney's secretary, they had at the very most forty-five minutes before Wesley would be a free man.

He opened the glove compartment and pulled out his Glock. He removed it from the holster and checked the magazine. It carried a full round of fifteen bullets. He hoped he wouldn't need to use them and if he had to, he prayed it would be enough.

Jillian would walk around the jail to the entrance where they would release him. She wanted to be there. He didn't like it. Wesley was a target; anybody near him became one by default. But, there was no convincing Jillian otherwise. So the best option entailed Ian picking them up in the car as quickly as he could and getting the hell out of Dodge.

During his walk to the parking garage, Ian decided that the best course of action would be to bring Wesley back to Matt and Stella's place. The remote location bought them some time to figure out their next move. Maybe if Greene acted quickly, whoever Wesley was making a deal with might come up with a protection plan for him.

His cell phone rang.

"Yeah."

"I'm here outside the entrance waiting," Jillian said. "Wesley isn't here, but it looks pretty quiet. Hardly anyone around."

Ian didn't say what was running through his mind, but every nerve crackled as his intuition told him that the absence of traffic, be it on foot or by car, might not be a good thing.

"Has Shawn or Matt called back?" Jillian asked.

"Not yet. Has Greene called?

"Yes, he was shocked and said he would contact the detective at Phoenix PD."

A short silence filled the air space. Then Jillian added, "I had hoped it would be the Feds and not the Phoenix police. I hope I'm wrong, but I thought the DEA just might be better equipped in keeping my brother safe."

"Looks like that's going to be our job," Ian replied. "I'm driving over now."

"Hurry, I'm expecting the door to open any minute and see Wes walking out."

Jillian disconnected the call. Ian turned on the ignition and fastened his seat belt. The cab of the car begin to close in. The semi-darkness of the garage and the reverberating echoes in the concrete structure added a sense of impending doom to his anxiety. *I have to get us through this. Jillian and Wesley depend upon me to keep them safe.* Ian sucked in slow breaths, held them and exhaled. Now was not the time for one of his flashbacks. He needed to be here and in the moment.

"Get a grip. You can do this," he whispered before he put the car into reverse and slowly pulled out of the parking place. As he carefully made his way out of the multi-level parking facility, the afternoon daylight filled the car's inside, and the tension across his back and shoulders eased.

The phone rang. *Jillian.* He picked up.

"We're here. Where are you?"

"Two blocks down and should be there in 30 seconds if I make the one stop light ahead."

"Good." The concern in her voice was palpable. "Oh, I see your car down the street."

He glanced and he saw her in the distance at the curb, waving. "Where's Wes?"

"He's back near the wall."

"Okay." Given what they were afraid would happen, hanging back out of sight was a smart move. The light at the one intersection ahead of him turned red.

"Damn," he growled as he pulled to a stop.

A crossover SUV pulled up to the intersection and made a left turn and headed down the street ahead of them. The vehicle was in the inside lane, and Ian could see Jillian ahead of him. Slowly Wesley walked to stand next to his sister on the right side of the street.

"No, not yet, Wes," Ian murmured.

The SUV continued down the road and then appeared to slow down. Ian blinked. Was this it? Someone's hand appeared out the passenger side window. Just as Ian thought he saw a weapon, gunfire cracked into the afternoon. Jillian and Wesley scrambled for cover behind a parked car.

"Dear God, no." Ian punched the accelerator, ran the light and picked up speed to close the gap on the SUV. He pulled up next to the SUV in the inside lane and skidded to a halt alongside the driver's side door. He shoved the transmission into park, pulled his Glock, shoved open the driver's door, stood and fired one shot into the cab of the SUV. The glass front windshield shattered.

The driver looked at him. His face went from surprise to panic in a second as he screamed to the man on the passenger side. As Ian raced across the front of his car, he had a view through the windshield and fired two more shots at the passenger. Ian's shooter recoiled and crumbled as the driver punched the SUV's accelerator and tried to pull away. As they passed, Ian came forward and fired at the driver. More glass shattered on the driver's side, but the man pulled away and the vehicle accelerated in the opposite direction.

The distance between him and the SUV increased. When he was sure that they were not going to double back or shoot, he looked over at the back entrance of the building. Jillian remained crouched down behind a car.

"Jillian!" Ian shouted.

"Here!" she yelled back as she slowly looked above the car she had hid behind and looked frantically around.

"Wes, are you…" Jillian started to ask.

"I'm okay," Wesley shouted.

Without a further word, Jillian rose and broke into a full run to Ian. As she neared, he set the weapon on the hood of his car and opened his arms. Jillian slammed into him, crushing him in a full body hug.

"Ian, I was so scared," she whispered with a distinct tremble in her voice.

Ian practically crushed her in his arms he held her so tightly. *She's fine. Unharmed. Okay.* The thoughts rolled through his mind. Slowly the waves of adrenaline washed away and he started to relax.

Jillian clung to him and buried herself into his chest. His hand rose to softly stroke her hair, and as the minutes passed, she gradually stopped shaking and eventually raised her head.

The exit's heavy metal door opened and the police came out with guns drawn. Wesley shouted at them, giving them a blow-by-blow recap of what had occurred.

Jillian gradually pulled back and Ian looked down at her. She wanted more time to be sure about this second chance, but he could see it in her eyes. She loved him.

He cupped his hand under her chin and kissed her and when they finally pulled back, they both were out of breath.

"We better go see how your brother is doing," Ian said softly.

Jillian nodded, swung around, and tucked herself under his arm as they walked back to where her brother and three officers stood.

"They're putting out an order to look for the SUV," Wesley announced as they neared the building's exit. "I hope they don't get away."

The young man threaded his hand through his hair and then crossed his arms. He looked back at the officer. "What do I do now?"

"We'll need you to come back in and make a statement, for starters."

Wesley's jaw dropped and Ian struggled not to laugh. The situation wasn't funny. Maybe it was just a release of nervous energy, but Jillian's brother's expression of shock and indignation struck him as hysterical.

The officer threw him a stern look. "You can go park your car by the curb, turn over your weapon and come in to make a statement as well."

"Yes sir," Ian said as he slowly disentangled himself from Jillian's grasp and walked back to his car.

They were going to be here awhile.

CHAPTER THIRTY-TWO

Two weeks later...

Jillian added a light coat of lip gloss and fluffed her hair. She paused to study her reflection in the mirror and noted that finally after several nights of restful sleep, her exhausted, sleep-deprived look had faded away. Ian would arrive soon and they'd go for a casual dinner with Shawn and his girlfriend, Morgan.

The image of Ian in front of the police station was never far from surfacing in her thoughts. Now, more than ever, she could understand why Ian had been troubled with nightmares. Strange, Jillian always thought that war battle was like some World War II movie where the boundaries between two armies was cleanly divided. Now she knew how deadly events could turn within a matter of seconds. Ian had saved her and Wes' lives.

The flat tire coupled with the wound the shooter had sustained had made them easy to capture. While they had been in the station providing statements, the police had found and taken the perpetrators into custody. The driver went straight to a holding cell and the shooter went into surgery before he was released from the hospital and jailed.

Wesley had made good on his deal with the narcotics task force by providing damning evidence on Rossi and his wide range of illegal activities. He was now in police protection at some undisclosed location, and she had not seen him in days. When he had called earlier this afternoon, he reported that Rossi was on the run.

A soft knock on the front door signaled Ian's arrival. She opened the door. He stood there in jeans, a white button-down shirt with the sleeves rolled up, and leather loafers.

"You're late," she said with a soft laugh.

He grinned back. "Been a crazy day."

"Ditto. So much for the normal routine we kept promising and hoping for." She walked over, wrapped her arms around his neck, and kissed him. Ian rested his hands on her hips and after she broke the kiss and leaned back, he gently reeled her in close.

"Again," he whispered.

She smiled and tilted her head up as he reclaimed her lips. His mouth was gentle, persuasive, and after a couple of long kisses, she pulled back a little breathless. "We have to go. If not, we'll be late. Do you know where the restaurant is?"

"Sort of. Shawn gave me the address. It's in north Scottsdale."

Jillian looked down at her jeans and silky tunic top. "Am I too casual?"

"Nope. Morgan says it's not a typical fancy Scottsdale establishment, but the Mexican food is first rate."

Ian allowed her to slide from his grip.

"Let me get my purse and lock up," she said softly.

Ian followed her into her front entry and waited. Jillian went back to her bedroom and, as she picked up the small leather handbag on her bed, she heard Simon meow.

The Siamese must have descended from his cat perch and, while approaching Ian, was definitely giving him an earful of demands to be petted, scratched, and acknowledged. She entered the living room, stopped, and watched as the cat wound himself around Ian's jeans, and Ian bent down and scratched the cat's back.

"Hey, buddy. How are you handling being back at home?"

Jillian smiled and raised her hand to her lips for a second to hide her smile. "Ready?"

Ian straightened. "I'll drive."

Jillian approached and turned on a lamp by the front entry. She ordered Simon, "You be good while I'm gone."

***

Thirty-five minutes later they entered Rosa's restaurant up at Pinnacle Peak and Scottsdale road. The Friday night crowd was out in force, and Ian patrolled the parking lot for several minutes before locating a place to park. After he locked the car, he walked around the hood and took her hand, threading his fingers through hers.

As they neared the outdoor patio, the smell of fajitas grew stronger, along with the boisterous noise from the crowd that waited outside the entrance for their table.

Jillian scanned the crowd, hoping to find Shawn. "Are we here first?"

Ian turned and grinned at her. "Hey, we're talking about my brother here. He's Mr. 'be there ten minutes ahead of time.'"

Jillian nodded and let Ian lead them through the crowd of people. Once inside the entry, the noise actually picked up a level. Ian walked up to the counter and checked to see if there was a "Randall" on the waiting list. The young hostess checked his clipboard and nodded. "Party of four, right?"

"Yes," Ian replied.

She smiled. "I believe they are in the bar."

"Thanks." Ian released Jillian's hand and cupped the small of her back. "Shall we?"

A couple in the back of the bar sat close together and appeared to be in intimate conversation. A pang gently punched at Jillian's gut. They looked so happy and in sync with each other, and she and Ian were about to interrupt that.

As if they sensed they were being watched, they both stopped talking and glanced at her and Ian.

"Come on," Ian urged and, when Jillian hesitated, he again took her hand. The brunette at the table caught Ian's gesture and a small, almost amused smile broke on her lips. As they approached, Shawn stood.

"Hey, you're late," his brother announced in a joking voice.

"No, you're early. As always," Ian quipped back.

The two brothers hugged and after they stepped back, Ian pulled out a chair next to Shawn's girlfriend and urged Jillian to sit.

"Jillian, meet Morgan," Ian said.

'Hi. Nice to meet you." Jillian forced a nervous smile and she extended her hand.

Morgan beamed back, and took her hand and squeezed it gently. "No, the pleasure is mine."

She withdrew her hand and glanced over to Ian. "You look good. How are things going?"

Jillian didn't miss the real questions behind the short, innocent-sounding sentence. Morgan looked genuinely interested in his answer, and Jillian decided immediately that she liked Morgan.

"I'm doing fine." He glanced over at Jillian briefly and then back at Shawn's girlfriend. "It's all good."

Suddenly a puzzled look graced his face as he looked down at Morgan's hand. For two, maybe three seconds, he stared at a glittering diamond ring and then a smile erupted on his face. "Is this what I think it is?"

He looked at Morgan and then back at his brother.

"Surprise!" Morgan laughed.

"I need a hug from my future sister-in-law."

Morgan rose from the chair and Jillian stood up so Ian could give Morgan a big hug. "You do know what you're getting yourself into, don't you?" Ian joked as he released his hug.

"Yep," Morgan answered. "But so do you."

"Yes," Ian whispered.

"Congratulations," Jillian offered.

Morgan opened her arms and gave Jillian a hug as well. As she pulled back, she grinned. "I understand that you own a place where you can have weddings."

Thank you for reading Exit Wounds. If you did enjoy it, please help others find this book by

- Sharing this book with a friend. Lending is enabled on this digital book.
- Recommending this friends.
- Writing a review on Amazon.com, Barnes and Noble, iBooks or Kobo. Reader reviews are high helpful in assisting those who are considering a book.

To find out about upcoming releases, contests, and special bonus material available:

- Sign up for my newsletter.
- Or like me on Facebook.

For more information about books by Taylor Michaels, please visit: www.taylormichaels.com.

Made in the USA
Columbia, SC
24 July 2018